Also by Lazarus Barnhill
From Indigo Sea Press

The Medicine People

Lacey Took a Holiday
The Mountain Woman Romance Series, 1

Caddo Creek
The Mountain Woman Romance Series, 2

East Light
Also contains *Charlie Cherry's Ninth Step*

indigoseapress.com

Pastor Larsen and the Church Rat

By

Lazarus Barnhill

Deep Indigo Books
Published by Indigo Sea Press
Winston-Salem

Deep Indigo Books
Indigo Sea Press
302 Ricks Drive
Winston-Salem, NC 27103
This book is a work of fiction. Names, characters,
locations and events are either a product of the author's
imagination, fictitious or used fictitiously. Any resemblance
to any event, locale or person, living or dead, is purely
coincidental.

For information regarding bulk purchases of this book,
digital purchase and special discounts, please contact the publisher
at indigoseapress@gmail.com

Cover design by Stacy Castanedo

Manufactured in the United States of America
ISBN 978-1-63066-450-3

Pour l'ange qui surprendra par sa descente.

Chapter One

Larsen could hear Horace walking down the hallway toward the minister's study. His footsteps, as always, slowed and grew softer as Horace got closer. And, as always, the custodian opened the door first and then knocked on it.

"Good Monday morning, Pastor."

Larsen, who had stopped reading the reports on his desk when he heard Horace approaching, nodded and returned the greeting. "How are you, Horace?"

"Fine, thanks." He stepped inside office and closed the door, wearing a conspiratorial expression. "Say, Pastor, I have something to tell you. Something I figured you'd want to know."

"What's that?"

His voice dropped off as if sharing a secret. "There's a rat in the church, Pastor."

He nodded again. "Yes. I heard something about that after the late service yesterday."

"The Loyal Men and Women's Class were the ones who saw it, Pastor. It zipped out from beneath the piano against the far wall—the one beneath the portrait of old Pastor Ulreich—right into the hallway and then disappeared."

"Yes. They say it was a pretty good sized rodent. No mistaking it for a mouse." He paused, waiting for Horace to continue. "Well, what do you think we should do about it?"

"Oh, I already put the traps out. Baited 'em with apples and peanut butter. Rats like that a lot better than cheese, you know. I don't think rats give a hoot-and-holler for cheese. Peanut butter, though, that draws 'em like a siren's song. They can't resist it."

"How many traps did you bait?"

"Three, Pastor. Really I suspect the one in the kitchen will get him. But I'm giving him a couple other options since I don't know exactly where in the church he's hiding out."

"So you think you'll trap him before next Sunday's service?"

"Oh, long before then. I'll catch him before choir practice on Wednesday."

"Well, that's good, Horace. I believe we're going to have a fair number of folks in and out of the church building this week. Do you think we should alert everyone as to the locations of these traps—you know, so nobody accidentally steps on one?"

Horace frowned. "Everyone? I don't think that's good idea, Pastor. Now I did tell Edith. I told her when I emptied her trash. And you should know about the rat and the traps—I mean, you are the pastor. But, honestly, Pastor, I don't think it's a good idea for us to announce this to the whole congregation—for a couple reasons. First off, some of the kids may decide to monkey with the traps. You know how kids are. And second, I don't think we want folks generally knowing that we have a rat."

He studied Horace's face closely. "So do you think it implies that something is spiritually wrong in the church if it has a rat, or is it just bad for evangelism?"

The custodian smiled. "I'm not theologian, Pastor—even though I've hardly missed a Sunday since I was a kid. I went through confirmation with old Pastor Stern, you know." He glanced at the ceiling thoughtfully. "And I don't remember that the Small Catechism says anything about rats being sinful. I just think on general principles we should keep our rodent issues on the 'QT'."

"You're probably right, Horace. And if you catch him before choir practice, there won't be much to tell anyway."

"Can I get your trash, Pastor?"

"Thanks, Horace. Would you please close the door on the way out?"

The custodian walked around behind the desk, making sure to glance at the papers spread before Pastor Larsen as he replaced the half full plastic bag in the waste basket. He started toward the door, pausing with one hand on the handle and looking back toward Larsen.

"Say, Pastor, I heard we got another one 'circling the drain.'"

"Excuse me?"

"Yeah. Jewel Vonnegut. I heard they moved her from Barnes-Jewish Hospital to hospice."

"Well . . . that's true." He labored, searching for the proper response. "I guess I wouldn't describe her as 'circling the drain' though. I might say 'she's in grave condition.' Maybe that just

2

sounds a little more appropriate."

Horace nodded, wearing his conspiratorial expression once more. "I know you have to say things like that from the chancel, Pastor. But between you and me, Jewel's fading into the sunset."

He gazed at the custodian. "True enough. She is not long for this world." Involuntarily he set his jaw. "I guess I need to finish this. It's for the synod. Good luck with the rat."

"Oh he's not going to be much of a problem, Pastor." Horace shifted his weight, leaning against the half-open door. "One other thing, Pastor. Me and the missus agreed the other day that you did a good job with Joanie's funeral last week. Funerals seem to be a calling card of yours, Pastor. My Mitzi says she hopes you'll be around long enough to do her funeral."

"Well, thank you for that compliment. Please tell Mitzi that I find it extremely unlikely I will do her funeral, since she's in excellent health and will probably dance on my grave."

Horace tilted his head broadly. "Well, I hope that's so, Pastor, but we're no spring chickens. And Mitzi has that tribulation, you know."

He looked back to the documents before him as he spoke. "Isn't it fibrillation? Atrial fibrillation?"

"It's her heart. Skips beats. Beats fast. That's not good."

"Well," he responded slowly, "I suspect, if the doctors get alarmed, they'll put in a pacemaker. Mitzi's going to outlive us all."

"Say Pastor."

Larsen looked up at him again.

"What'd you think of Joanie's daughter?"

He had prepared himself for that very question and showed no emotion. "Beats me, Horace. Had you ever heard before Joan died that she had a daughter?"

"No. We knew Joanie as long as she belonged to St. Timothy's—fifteen years. And I don't remember her ever mentioning she had any family. Then she dies and this daughter shows up from Florida."

"Well Ms. Celeste is legitimately Joan's heir. She had all the documentation to prove she was Joan's daughter. And Joan had listed her as next of kin and put her contact information in the advance directives."

3

"The what?"

"Advance directives. You know, if you go into a coma or you have a stroke and you can't tell the doctors and hospitals and nursing homes what you want. You make a lot of decisions beforehand—"

"Oh, a living will."

"Yeah. A living will."

The conspiratorial look appeared again. "That daughter was kind of a looker, don't you think?"

Larsen shrugged. "If you say so, Horace. When you're a pastor and you're arranging a funeral right after a sudden death, you don't have a lot of opportunities just to enjoy the view, if you know what I mean."

Horace shrugged. "Is the daughter still around here?"

"I guess." He focused again on the paperwork before him. "When somebody dies suddenly like that, there are a lot of loose ends that have to be cleared up. I don't know if that will involve the church or not, but I suspect Ms. Celeste will have to stick around Alton for a few days at least."

". . . Didn't exactly look like the church-going type, did she?"

Larsen shrugged again. "Maybe that's how people dress for church in Florida. They're a little more casual down there than they are in St. Louis."

"Well, I got to get back to work, Pastor."

"Okay. See you later."

After the door latched, Larsen leaned back in his swivel chair. Seconds passed. He heard Horace's step retreating down the hall.

He gazed around himself at the dark walnut paneled study, lined with copiously burdened bookshelves and the paraphernalia of the pastoral ministry. Cranberry colored curtains covered the single window in the office. This day, like most days, Larsen kept the curtains closed. The window was simply a visual portal to the church narthex, the busiest room in the building. The window into his office, he had decided soon after he came to St. Timothy's, was more for church members to keep an eye on the pastor than to let in any light.

It was at that particular moment—as he was trying to give a name to the unpleasant, distressed and disgusted emotional state in which he found himself—his cell phone rang. More precisely, it

4

began to play the first few notes of "A Mighty Fortress Is Our God," the ringtone installed on it by his younger daughter Daphne, and which he kept forgetting to replace. The caller ID read "A Celeste." He pressed the green dot on the screen and held the phone to his ear.

"Hello."

"Pastor Larsen. This is Ange Celeste. How are you?"

"I'm good. How are you?"

"Excellent."

The silence that followed went on so long he began to think she was expecting him to say something. Then she spoke again.

"So I've been going through Mother's stuff. I've discovered a few more things I think you might like. . . . Interested?"

He nodded. "Absolutely."

"Wonder when you can drop by?"

Larsen sighed, thinking over his daily agenda. What did he most want to cancel?

"How about just after lunch? About 1:30 or 1:45."

"Works for me. You remember the way?"

"I do."

"Okay. See you, Pastor Larsen." The phone went dead.

The despair he had been feeling was gone. In its place was a feeling he found far more exciting. And dangerous.

The river was up. Crossing the Mississippi on the Highway 67 bridge, Larsen gazed upstream and then down. The turbulent water raged around all obstacles, natural and man-made, in its broad path. Whatever romance he had imputed to the great river had gradually disappeared over his five years of living and working in proximity to it, observing its relentless, overwhelming, muddy current. The ocean—all oceans—had the good sense to retreat twice a day, to have times of robust churning interspersed with placid, nearly motionless periods. The river, on the other hand, seemed only to alternate between low filthiness and high murkiness. There were those occasions, he had been told, when it was especially heinous, when it threatened its levied banks.

"When the river gets really high, Pastor," someone in the church had told him, "be glad you live in West County."

He was glad, at this moment, to be rid of west St. Louis

5

County, rid of Missouri and the church and the pastoral ministry. For an hour or perhaps two, Martin Luther Larsen had respite. And the realization of it made him think of that to which he was escaping—of her to whom he was escaping. He drew a deep, uncertain breath and remembered his first visit to Ange Celeste at her mother's townhouse.

She had answered the door shoeless, wearing a close-fitting black dress and no makeup. Her black hair was just long enough to bounce when she let him in the front door and immediately turned toward the kitchen table, where packets of documents and possessions were stacked. He assumed she was going to hand him the items she had promised him at the funeral and bid him farewell, until he saw the magnum of red wine and the two glasses beside it. First he thought he would have to turn down the offered drink, and then he wondered if perhaps he should not have assumed. Perhaps she was expecting other company. She sat down in one of the two chairs at the table and crossed her bare legs.

"Can you sit down for a minute? It was nice of you to come all the way out here to pick these things up, Pastor Larsen," she said.

He pulled out the chair and sat down. The daughter sat in the one he had always used in past visits. It was strange to him to sit in the chair Joan Celeste sat in when he visited her, where she graciously offered him crumb cake and lemonade.

"I came out here to Alton a lot, actually. Your mother was very dear to me. That is, she was just as nice and hospitable as she could be. And I always really appreciated that. I enjoyed coming to visit her." He smiled. "Of course you mother very faithfully showed up every Sunday. It's a long way from Alton to Manchester. But she never missed. When someone comes that far every week, you want to show your appreciation."

Ange Celeste stared at him. It was a bit disconcerting to Larsen. Did she not believe that he visited often, or did she doubt his sentiments? Did she—perhaps cynical about church life or even an outright disbeliever—look down on the sort of pastoral relationship he described? The unexpected or incomprehensible reactions of extremely attractive women had always troubled him, made him feel like an unappealing buffoon.

"She liked you."

Her words and the way she spoke them surprised him. It was

almost like a pronouncement or a verdict Joan had handed down for her daughter to share with Larsen in her absence. And there was something about the tone she used. It was wiser and perhaps more intimate than he expected.

"Well. I liked her."

"She told me about conning you into going to the fall festival here in Alton. And on a Saturday, no less. And she told me about your favorite wine."

Without asking, she turned and grasped the magnum in two hands. Larsen's mouth dropped. He stammered, started to protest that he was working, had other appointments to keep that Friday afternoon and could not drink. The daughter paid no attention to him, though, as she poured the glasses full.

"A nice Nebbiolo from *Verità Wino*, your favorite Italian winery."

". . . I really shouldn't."

She had anticipated his reluctance and brushed it aside. "One glass, Pastor Larsen. Only 12% alcohol. Undetectable." She picked up the glasses and handed one to him. "A toast to my mother, the divine Joan Celeste."

He laughed, somewhat anxiously, as they touched their glasses. "To Joan."

The wine was as he remembered it: rosy and slightly tart with a lingering mellow aftertaste. And with the first taste he felt himself begin to relax. The second and third sips did not disappoint.

"I did not know *Verità Wino* produced a magnum size of their Nebbiolo."

She looked at the bottle, as if seeing it for the first time. "Well I guess they do." She smiled at him. "Mother said it was ironic that you liked this wine."

He gazed at her. "Seriously? Why did she say that?"

"Because you are so much like it."

"What?"

"The Nebbiolo grape takes an exceptionally long time from the moment it blooms until it's ready to pluck." She smiled. "And once you do skin it and start the fermentation process, it takes a very long time before . . . it's ready for the bottle."

He stared at her oval face, cream-colored complexion, dark

7

almond eyes, pert nose and small mouth. She bore only the faintest resemblance to her mother, whom he had only known in her 70's. How old was this daughter? Forty perhaps, at most? Was she a late-life child?

"What does that have to do with me?"

She had finished her glass and poured another. "I guess Mother thought you were a work-in-progress." She grabbed his glass in his hand and steadied it as she brought the neck of the magnum onto the lip and filled it again.

"No thanks. . . . Uh. What did your mother mean, that I'm a 'work-in-progress?' Was I not the pastor she needed me to be?"

"I seriously doubt that, Pastor Larsen. . . . Sounds like you worry about that kind of thing though." She took another drink.

He thought about it. "Every pastor worth his salt wants to be the shepherd his—or her—congregation needs."

"How politically correct of you."

He laughed. "Heaven knows I try, Ms. Celeste."

"Ange"

"Ang?"

"No. Say it right. It's pronounced 'auhnjj.' It's French."

"Ange."

"That's right."

"Well, Ange, I take it you don't have a great deal of use for church life and customs."

Her head tipped to one side. "I don't do religion the way my mother did. That doesn't mean I'm not spiritual."

Larsen chuckled. For the first time since he came through the door, he felt himself on solid footing. "That's the mantra of the age, isn't it, Ms. Cel—Ange? I keep hearing people say they aren't religious. They're spiritual. I've begun to think that's supposed to be a free pass from living out a rigorous life of faith."

"Aren't you the preacher?" She tittered. "Is it possible people tell you they're spiritual and not religious as a nice way of saying, 'I don't have to join your church to know God just as much as I want or need'?"

He had to stop and think about her question. "Does anybody ever have as much God as they need? I don't think I do. And I'm not sure saying 'I'm spiritual, not religious,' is anything more than a deflection. At least for—" How could he express it? "—some of

8

the people who say it. Present company excepted. . . . So, were you raised in the church as a child, and then drifted away as an adult? If you don't mind me asking."

She set her glass on the table and produced, from a drawer in the edge of the table he had not seen, a cigarette. "I've been in and out of churches for as long as I can remember. . . . Relax, Pastor Larsen. It's a vape. I promise you won't smell like cigarettes."

". . . So you are a spiritual seeker?"

"No." She leaned forward, an elbow on a bare knee, a scant twelve inches from his crossed legs. "I just always seem to fall in love with seekers. . . . But you aren't a spiritual seeker, are you Pastor? You're a guide."

Larsen had to force himself not to look at her crossed bare legs. He tried to decide if there was a hint of cynicism in her voice. It wasn't sincerity he was hearing. She seemed to be playing with him.

"Your last name is Celeste, like your mom. So, may I ask if you are single? Or divorced? Do you have children?" He swallowed a full drink of the Nebbiolo. "That's the great thing, you see, about being a pastor. You get to ask all these personal questions. People assume it's your ministerial privilege."

She inhaled a puff of electronic smoke and held it in her lungs for long seconds. "I'm not married. I have no children."

"Is this interfering with your career—having to come to St. Louis—well, Alton—like this and stick around to settle your mother's estate?"

"Well I'm a counselor," she said. "A psychotherapist. So for the time being I've turned my clients over to other counselors until Mom's estate is settled. Then when I return to Florida, I get all my crazies back, plus a few extra when my colleagues need me to return the favor."

"Don't you worry that some of them will get well without you?" As soon as he had asked it, he realized it was a hideous, spiteful question. He had tried to be playful and it came out hateful.

She gazed at him. Something like admiration shone behind her eyes. "Really, Pastor Larsen, what if your parishioners find their way God without you? Wasn't it a bishop who said to his subordinates: 'Remember, boys, a saved world puts us out of business'?"

"Touché, Ms. Celeste. I had that coming. Allow me to blame the wine for saying such a stupid thing. In reality, however, my denomination in general and I in particular aren't much into the whole salvation-damnation thing. Our perspective is that God has already accomplished salvation through the sacrifice of Christ on the cross. Our task is not so much to warn people of the need for God's grace as to demonstrate to them how to respond to it, how to live transformed lives through experiencing the reality of God's eternal love in a mortal world."

She studied his face, not so much as if trying to decide how to respond, but rather with a look of yearning. "Here's something I've never understood, Pastor. If God figured out how to cleanse all humanity of its sin and change the destiny of the whole human race in one fell swoop 2000 years ago, how come God has so much trouble getting denominations or churches or even just individual Christians to act any differently than they would if there were no cross or church or God? Wait!" She held up hand like a stop sign. "Let me guess. Free will? People have to decide for themselves to receive and be changed by God's grace."

"Something like that."

She nodded. She leaned forward and rubbed her hands on either side of the leg sitting atop the other, and when she did, Larsen saw her breasts, perfectly shaped orbs, dangling, dark-nippled, unconcealed and unconstrained by a brassiere. The view filled him with an instant of arousal, followed by alarm. The little inner monologue that always reminded him of his professional, ethical responsibilities whispered that he needed to ignore the casual, marvelous attractiveness of this woman. It was in his best interest, the voice said briskly, to conclude the intoxicating visit, take the documents she had promised him and be on his way.

He emptied his glass of wine with a swallow and set it on the table. "Thank you so much, Ms. Ange Celeste. It has been stimulating and challenging to get to know you."

Her eyes serenely half-lidded, she ignored his declaration of farewell. "Mother said you're married to a teacher."

On the other hand he truly enjoyed this marvelous woman and her unpredictability. After all, nothing was going to happen between them. It never did. He had himself under control and his defenses were sure. She might even be one of those who sought to

10

titillate a clergyman until he responded in kind—only to pretend to be offended.

". . . Yes. Mary-Martha. She teaches high school English and social studies over in West County."

"And you have two daughters?"

He smiled. "Donna, my eighth grader. She is the embodiment of her mother. She looks like Mary-Martha and they have the very same personality. And then there is Daphne, my sixth grader. Thank god she looks just like me. Otherwise there would be no reason to believe she's mine. She is the most precocious, mischievous, ironic and playful child in creation."

The daughter smiled. "Maybe she is the way you would be if you didn't have to wear the pastor's costume all the time."

She didn't intend it in an insulting way, he decided. She was being playful. Perhaps even teasing. He wondered if she realized how alluring she was, if she actually meant to be.

"Hmm," he said. "Well, just maybe there is a difference between a costume one wears to present a front to the world and the cloth one adopts to make a difference in the world."

She giggled. "You're so poetic. Is that the first time you said that bullshit or have you practiced it? I know that's why Mom loved to hear you talk. Still, regardless of whether it's a costume or a calling, it's pretty hard for little Marty to come out and play isn't it?"

"Huh. And do you ever stop being the psychologist, Miss Ange? I was an inhibited guy before I ever made it to the pastoral ministry. The cloth just happens to fit. There's another old saying: 'God can strike a mighty blow with a crooked stick.'"

"How 'bout with a straight arrow?" she came right back.

He rose. "I should be getting back across the river."

"Sure," she said, opening the little drawer in the table and stashing her electronic smoke. "I have Mom's church stuff set aside here. Before you go, would you be willing, Pastor, to reach something for me?"

"Reach something?"

"It's a box at the back of her closet." She picked up the chair she had been sitting on and walked into Joan's bedroom, calling back to him. "I can't reach it, even standing on a chair. I suspect Mom accidentally pushed it back here and then never could get it."

11

Larsen stood at the table, filled with wariness. "What's in this box?"

Just her head appeared from the bedroom door, a coy smile on her face. "I have no idea what's hidden there. That's why I need you to help me retrieve it—so I can see what's in it. Probably romance novels, knowing Mom." When he made no move toward her, she said, "Tell you what, if there are negotiable bonds or equity stocks or Confederate dollars in it, I'll give your church a tithe. Deal?"

He sighed. "I'm glad to get the box for you. And the church doesn't want your mom's money."

"Well—" She disappeared into the bedroom. "—it's mine now, isn't it?"

It was his first time in Joan Celeste's bedroom. As with the rest of her apartment, it was adorned in colors of peach and rust, and consummately neat—almost as if Joan had tidied it that morning. The bed was covered with an abundance of pillows and a thick bedspread, pulled back to reveal the off-white sheets beneath. Ange had not made the bed after the last time she slept in it. And the daughter's suitcases sat against the far wall—one closed and upright, the other flat and open with clothing protruding. He turned away, so as not to see intentionally what clothes were spread there. It was an altogether strange experience for him to be in the most private room of his deceased parishioner—now the sleeping quarters of this woman he did not know at all. He felt oddly guilty and intrusive. And he found himself wondering what she wore to bed.

"Larsen," the daughter said to herself absently as she carried the wooden chair into the closet. "You must be Scandinavian."

"Swedish."

"That's pretty Scandinavian."

She had placed the chair all the way back in the walk-in closet and stood beside it in the dimness facing him. He turned on the light and stepped in, looking to the shelf at the farthest reaches of the closet.

"I would have guessed you were Swedish. Or Norwegian. Or Danish. What with the blond hair and blue eyes. . . . And what are you, six foot?"

"Ha." He smiled. "Five ten."

"Well, short as you are, you should still be able to reach Mother's treasure."

". . . Where is it?"

She patted the back rest of the chair. "Stand on here and you can see it."

He wheeled the chair around so the front of his legs would press against the chair back and give him support, then stood on the seat. There was indeed a box, small and cube-shaped, sitting so far back against the wall that the woman could not have reached it.

"Yeah, you're right."

He grasped it, barely, and scooted it toward him until he could pick it up. It was wrapped almost like a gift, in dusty tissue paper and bound with a ribbon that once had been red. As he straightened, his balance shifted and for an instant he thought he would fall. The woman, standing beside the chair, instantly put her arms around his legs, her breasts pressed against his thighs, to steady him.

"You all right?"

"Yeah. . . . You can let go. I can get down."

He held onto the hanger bar and stepped down. When he did, he was face to face with Ange, looking down at her flawless face. Larsen handed the package to her and eased down to sit on the chair sideways.

"You sure you're all right?"

"A little dizzy for a minute." He put his hand to his forehead. "Maybe a little disoriented. Not used to drinking wine in the afternoon. Just give me a second."

". . . However long you need, Pastor. You're the one in a hurry."

He sighed. "I'm sorry I've come across that way, Ange. Really, I just don't to give you the wrong idea."

". . . The wrong idea about what?"

"I mean." He rubbed his forehead, his eyes closed. "When you are a person in my profession, sometimes you find yourself alone in close quarters with very attractive women. And you have to make sure you maintain your . . . ethical boundaries."

"This happens to you a lot, does it?"

"What? No. Not really."

She nodded, her voice condescending. "Well I'm glad you

prepared yourself for it when it finally did. . . . You think I'm attractive?"

Larsen had no idea how to respond. He had no idea how to respond in professional, ethical way at least.

She smiled down upon him. "And now you're speechless. All alone in a bedroom closet with a willing woman. . . . And you have no idea what to say or do? . . . Do you need a hint?"

He looked up at her. She was still so very close to him, her legs touching his. And he could not only smell her breath, but feel it in the proximity. With no word of warning, she lifted one hand and cradled his chin in it. Then she bent forward and, with excruciating slowness, brought her lips to his and kissed him. The kiss was at once horrifying and completely exhilarating. He should resist, he thought. But he didn't.

She sat across his lap then, her legs around his hips, and ran her free hand back through his sandy hair. Pressing her face to his, she kissed him again. Now it was his own breathing he sensed.

"I . . . haven't kissed a woman . . . romantically . . . since I got married."

She smiled. "Well, apart from what you just admitted about your wife, I would say you're overdue." And she kissed him again, hard, slipping her tongue between his lips. "I want to ask you a question."

Warnings fired within his mind, overruled by curiosity and the beautiful strangeness of the experience. "What?"

"Well, what was it you were thinking when you first came through the door? You gave me such a strange look."

He swallowed. "Well . . . I was thinking, 'That must be the famous little black dress I've always heard about.'"

"Uh-hmm. And what did you think when I bent forward at the table while ago and you saw my girls?"

"Ha! . . . So you realized that? . . . I thought they were beautiful. Perfect."

She straightened a little on his lap. "Really? You think so?"

Without another word or moving more than to lift her delicious bottom from his lap, she raised her arms and pulled the dress up and over her head. And there they were, round and flawless and only inches from his face—only now the nipples protruded in arousal. She wrapped her arms around him and pressed her naked breasts against him.

"It's so very nice to be appreciated, Marty." She leaned away from him. "See anything else you like?"

Glancing down, he realized she had been completely unclothed beneath the dress. A tiny triangle of dark pubic hair peeked from the intersection of her legs, until she gently eased them apart. She watched him as he gazed down at the tiny protuberance of her clitoris. Leaning forward again, she pressed one breast against his face. In accommodation, he took it fully in his mouth, putting his arms around her and pulling her against him. She put her hand on the back of his head, forcing his face against her bare chest. When he stopped to breathe, she kissed him again. They gazed at each other.

"What is that I feel? What am I sitting on that wasn't there a moment ago? . . . You have the better of me, Marty" she said. She stood, holding his hand. "You could at least come in here and show me what you look like under your clothes."

As Larsen pulled up to the complex where Joan Celeste had lived, the awareness of what had happened on his first visit to her daughter Ange—how he had, childlike, risen holding the woman's hand and followed her to the bed—and what was most certainly going to happen now, this very afternoon, coursed through him electrically.

"I believe you're right, Horace," he said quietly, turning off the Nissan. "We do have a rat in the church. I've seen him in the mirror."

Chapter Two

"You can make yourself some cereal, can't you?" Mary-Martha asked.

"Yeah. . . . Do we have anything that's not 100% sugar?"

"Depends on whether or not you believe what's written on the box."

"Yeah." He slid a cereal box back into the cupboard. "I think I'll stop on the way to church and get myself a bagel."

"Okay." She shrugged. "Comes out of your work budget though."

He glanced over his shoulder at her. She was completely made up and her hair was fixed, but she wore a bathrobe over her pajamas as she packed lunches into paper bags.

"Since when does breakfast come out of my work allowance?"

"Don't say 'allowance,' Martin. Makes it sound like you're a little boy." She folded shut the top of a lunch bag. "Breakfast comes out of your budget since you aren't eating food I bought for breakfast out of the family budget."

"Right. Do you think you can find money in the family breakfast budget for something an adult wants to eat for breakfast?"

She ignored his question and hastened around him to pull out the slow cooker. "We're having pot roast tonight," she said. "That's pretty grown up, isn't it?"

"Yes. I love pot roast. How come you only fixed two lunches today?"

Mary-Martha looked at him. "Donna isn't feeling well. She is staying home by herself."

"Oh. Okay, I guess."

"You don't mind calling her a couple times, do you? Just to check up on her."

"No. I'm glad to. Does she have cold or something?"

His wife stopped for another instant, drawing close to him. At first he thought he had said something stupid. Then he realized she didn't want anyone else in the house to overhear what she was saying.

16

"Your daughter started her first period last night."

Larsen straightened. "Oh. Oh my god. . . . Well. She's thirteen. I expect that's pretty much expected and normal."

Mary-Martha shook her head. "Not to her, it's not. Between the cramps and the bleeding, she believes her life is over. I told her she could take one day off from school. That's all the mercy the universe allows."

He leaned against the counter, thinking about his elder child. "Well. . . . Don't know what I should do."

"Nothing. That's what you should do. In fact, on second thought, don't even call her today. I will if I get a chance."

"Friend of mine sent his daughter a dozen roses when she had her first period. Sent a note that said, 'Congratulations. You are now a woman.'"

She stopped again, pointing a serving spoon at him. "You do that and your child will run you through a wood chipper. She doesn't want any sympathy, attention or conversation about this. Especially from her father."

He nodded. "Well. So much for being a caring dad."

"This is one of those times when caring means keeping your mouth shut."

"Yeah. . . . How will she know whether I'm caring or oblivious?"

She put the lid on the slow cooker and turned it on. "Just don't say anything. You can't make it better."

"Yeah. I'll tell you, living in this 'house of women' is a little perplexing. When I do nothing, it's wrong. And when I do something, it's wrong."

"Poor baby."

"How much simpler my life would have been if you'd just had boys. It's always easier to know what to do with them."

"Yeah right. That's what we needed was boys—like my little brothers. Constant contests to see who can fart loudest at the supper table." She laughed as she washed off the spoon and dropped it in the sink. "Sorry about your confusion, Martin. For me, two girls and a tubal was a sign of divine blessing." She disappeared through the kitchen door, calling back, "You're home after supper tonight, right?"

"Yep."

17

Larsen stood in the kitchen, alone, leaning against the counter, finishing his coffee. He could hear Mary-Martha climbing the stairs. Daphne was drying her hair in the girls' bathroom. Music was playing in Donna's bedroom. He sighed. With his entire family in the house, why did he feel so vaguely alone?

He rinsed the cup and went into his study to grab his backpack. For a few seconds he stood at the base of the staircase before deciding to climb up. He stopped outside Donna's bedroom door and tapped, loud enough for her to hear him above the music.

When she did not respond, he called without opening the door, "Donna."

". . . What?"

"Dad's going to work, sweetie. I'll call during the day to check on you." There was an interminable length of silence. "Hope you get to feeling—"

"Go away, Dad!"

Chastened, he descended the stairs, walked out the door to the Nissan in the driveway and got in.

He sat still with the motor running for a few seconds, hooking his mp3 player into the sound system and looking through the menu for some music that appealed to him. When "Rolling Stones" appeared in the viewer, he selected the tab and scrolled down until he found "Gimme Shelter." Backing out of the driveway, he meandered through the residential streets slowly in route to the bagel shop.

Martin Luther Larsen had to see himself in a different light now, he realized. For fifteen years as an ordained minister he had always shaken his head in wonder and disgust at ministerial colleagues—in and out of his denomination—who became involved in sexual liaisons. "Zipper problems," as an old bishop had called them, tainted a fair percentage of ministerial careers and also the congregations in which they occurred. It had always mystified him on those occasions when he knew the "correspondents" with whom the ministers were involved. They never seemed all that glamorous and it made him wonder what was so alluring about them that wise, mature, often deeply spiritual clergymen would risk losing so much for them. The answer that made the most sense to him was the one offered by a Bowen Theory lecturer he heard: the affairs and misconduct in which clergy engaged were actually smokescreens, explosive distractions from the ordinary misery of ministerial life, sure fire—if subconscious—methods for clergy to escape stressful, untenable pastorates and professions.

He chuckled. "Is that subconsciously what I'm trying to do, fuck myself out of the St. Timothy's? Maybe out of the ministry? Wouldn't it be a whole lot easier on everyone just to say, 'I can't take this anymore—I'm out of here'?"

The flaw in that theory, it occurred to him, was Ange herself. She was so appealing, so exuding of sexuality that no mature, lucid adult would ever wonder why he had fallen into bed with her. Indeed she was so attractive that Larsen knew he could not reveal he spent any time with her at all. He would immediately be suspected of having an affair with a woman like Ange if people knew he had frequent contact with her.

"On the other hand, if people knew I was around her a lot and didn't try to take her to bed, they'd wonder what the hell was wrong with me," he muttered.

It was the height of religious irony to him that, the very Sunday after he first made love to her, a rat had appeared in the church. He wondered about the prophetic portent of it. He felt beyond doubt that the Holy Spirit was confronting him, using his own guilty conscience to draw a comparison. In a spiritual sense, he knew, he was the real rat of St. Timothy's. Was he being confronted as well that, in the same inevitable way the rat would be trapped and discarded, so he would eventually be discovered and dispatched? Perhaps it was more warning than condemnation, God's way of saying: "Stop seeing the woman now and you'll avoid losing everything that's important to you, everything you've worked for."

He sat before the front door of the bagel shop, listening to the last strains of the song. "It's just a shot away. It's just a shot away."

"Bishop Johnson called yesterday afternoon while you were out making calls," Edith said.

"Oh." Larsen felt a momentary flush of panic. Why would Bishop Johnson have called when he was with Ange? "Am I supposed to call him back?"

"You don't have to," the secretary replied. "He really called for me, not you. I just thought you'd want to know."

". . .Okay. You mind me asking why he called?"

She didn't look up from the financial report she was entering into the computer. "He just had me add him to the Sunday worship bulletin."

Larsen felt his chin sag. "He put himself in the worship service? Without asking the pastor or the Worship Chair? What does he intend to do?"

Edith paused to look up at him, her expression one of patronizing patience. "He says he wants to make an announcement about the synod's district assembly here this fall and to ask for volunteers from the congregation."

His face flushed and his jaw instantly tightened. "Edith, as I explained to the good bishop, our council has not yet approved having the assembly here. It's only been a week since he asked us to host it and the Property Department hasn't even met to discuss it yet."

"Yes." She resumed typing. "I told him that."

"And what did he say?"

"He said St. Timothy's was overdue to host the district."

"Yeah, well," he tried to keep the anger out of his voice, "when he makes that announcement from the chancel, he's going to make it look I dropped the ball, that I was supposed to have everything already approved months ago. And why did he wait so late to ask? If he wanted to have the assembly here this year, he shouldn't have waited until Eastertide to ask. He should have asked way back in Advent before we did our annual planning retreat."

"Actually he did. Last Christmastide he asked Trinity Church to host this year's assembly."

"Trinity?" he said. "Then why is he asking us?"

"Trinity turned him down. So did St. Thomas." She looked up at him, her face cherubic. "You and I know how the bishop is. Nobody wants to work with him."

He gazed at her silently. It was, he knew, a ploy. Anything said in the church office about the district—and especially about the bishop—would go straight back to Richard Johnson. Anything he said—any negative thing—would be repeated to the bishop before noon.

"I got to get to work," he said.

"Don't forget the women this morning."

"What?"

"This is the Day Circle's monthly meeting."

"Oh that's right. The monthly 'State of the Congregation Address.'" He slipped quickly down the hall toward his office before the church administrator thought of some other reminder she needed to bestow upon him.

He dumped his backpack on the sofa and pushed aside his intentions so he could think of what he would say to the older ladies. The devotional should be something long enough to demonstrate he was really invested in it—something saccharine and comforting and definitely from the lectionary, for those women who worshipped it.

The "prayer report" he also had to give them at the meeting was much trickier. Each month there was an unspoken contest between him and the members of the Day Circle. They prided themselves on knowing precisely the physical condition and emotional state—as well as the current status of every relationship and career and family configuration—of every church member. By implication, if they knew a great deal more church gossip than Larsen did, it meant he had failed that month to be the shepherd of the flock; if he knew too much more than they did, then he wasn't sharing enough with these caring "prayer warriors." It was never easy, but it became most difficult when he knew something of great significance about a member or family within the church that had to be kept in absolute confidence. Their protestations of understanding aside, the Day Circle ladies had no grasp of the possibility—let alone importance—of privileged information.

He wrote down the names of church members who were "in need of prayer"—that was, those who had been in the hospital or crisis or such on-going stasis that they could be considered "homebound." Larsen shook his head wearily. Being homebound—at least, thank god, he had weaned the members from calling them "shut-ins"—didn't mean what he had first assumed it did.

He remembered anxiously standing on the porch of Mrs. Weaver's house, wondering what had happened to her, to what hospital she might have been transported, when her neighbor's car

21

pulled up and Mrs. Weaver climbed out quite ably, hustled past him and unlocked the front door.

"Hairdresser ran late," she had muttered.

Larsen stood on her step thinking the situation over. She was, he had been told from his first days at St. Timothy's, one of those unable to attend church. Other congregation members knew that, it was explained, because she simply had not been to the church in years. She did expect regular calls from the pastor, however. And when he was ten or fifteen minutes late—the result of other members being unwilling to let go of him so he could continue his visitation—Mrs. Weaver nagged and chastised him. What was the correct title, Larsen wondered, for a person who could make it to the hairdresser quite well, but was physically unable to make it to any church activity?

Five minutes before he was to appear before the Day Circle, the intercom buzzed.

"Yes, Edith."

"It's Rabbi Tushman."

"Oh. Thanks." He picked up the phone and leaned back in his swivel chair. "Hey, Sam. How's my favorite tush—or second favorite anyway?"

"I am good, Martin. How is my favorite blue-eyed Gentile."

He smiled. "I am able to sit up and take nourishment."

"That's a good thing. So when shall we do lunch?"

"Ugh. I'm socked in this week, Sam. How about . . . next Wednesday?"

There was the tapping sound over the receiver of the rabbi typing. "Got it on the calendar. Want to go down to the Loop? Have some gumbo?"

"Yeah. That sounds really nice."

"Well." Tushman shifted. "You know why I'm really calling there, don't you, Pastor?"

Larsen sighed. "You want to know if the council voted to join MOTION."

"Yes I do, Martin."

". . . I couldn't pull it off, Sam. The council voted against it."

To his credit, the rabbi didn't let the silence linger between them. "Well, Martin, I am sorry to hear that. I really had hopes they would join up. . . . This was only the first time they voted on

22

it, though. Maybe before long they'll reconsider."

He nodded. "It could happen, I suppose, Sam. According to our charter, I can't bring up a proposition that has been defeated for another twelve months."

Tushman laughed. "That sounds like something the synagogue would come up with."

"I don't think so. That sounds like the sort of repressed, overly cautious bullshit that's most characteristic of Christians."

"Um hmm. You might be amazed at how many rabbis get criticized by their congregations for not being Christian enough."

They chuckled. Larsen leaned forward, his elbows on his desk. "Don't feel bad about this, Martin."

"Hard not to, Sam. I really wanted to do the community organizing training. I thought maybe involving the church in local outreach would—I guess this sounds a little crazy, saying it to a rabbi—I was hoping it would make the church take the Gospel a little more seriously. . . . Did you have this trouble getting your people to sign on?"

"Yeah. I succeeded because I had a couple members who had done some serious mission work in Haiti after the earthquake. They were absolutely convinced we needed to be involved in making this a better place for everyone. Ultimately no one could disagree with them, and my agreeing with them made it happen. . . . But for you, I think you're kind of the Lone Ranger over there."

"Ha. I'm the voice crying in the wilderness, saying, 'We need to keep our town from becoming like North Saint Louis.'"

"Yeah, well I can tell you from experience, if you're waiting for the Messiah to show up, you better be prepared to be patient."

Chapter Three

Just before lunch he heard the familiar steps of Horace tracking down the hallway toward his study, the heaviness growing less and less as he approached. There was a momentary silence, then the door swung open halfway and the custodian knocked.

Horace seemed a bit surprised to see Larsen leaning back in this chair, staring at him. "Hi, Pastor. Happy Friday to you."

"Hello, Horace. What can I do for you?"

"Me? Nothing. I just wanted to update you that the whole church is clean as a whistle and ready for his holiness, the bishop, on Sunday."

"Thank you, Horace. You always do a good job. I'm sure the bishop will notice how immaculate things are and he'll appreciate it too, just as we all do."

Horace looked down. "Hope so, Pastor. There's just one thing."

"The rat?"

He shook his head, his face wearing undisguised frustration and shame. "I've doubled the number of traps and put fresh bait in them every day. I just haven't caught that big sucker."

"Maybe he's already split and headed over to the Presbyterians."

"No, that's just it. There's evidence of him here and there through the whole building. Big old rat droppings in the kitchen and choir room. I found a chewed candy wrapper in the balcony."

"You don't think that was from kids being messy?"

He shook his head. "No. Those ornery two-legged critters know how to tear into candy. They don't chew through the package."

Larsen nodded slowly. "What are we going to do about this rodent?"

"We're going to catch and kill him, Pastor," Horace said with conviction. "I'm taking this as a personal challenge now. It's me or that rat."

24

"Well—" His cell phone began its spiritless playing of its sacred ringtone. "—when you put it like that, I don't the rodent has a prayer." He glanced at "A. Celeste" on the little screen. "Excuse me, Horace. I need to take this."

The custodian showed no sign of leaving to give his pastor any privacy. Larsen pressed the phone tightly to his ear.

"Martin Larsen."

"Hello, Marty. You must not be able to talk right now."

"Oh, how are you? I'm in the middle of meeting at the moment. Can I call you back in five minutes?"

She laughed, exhaling at the same time. The sound was maddeningly erotic. Larsen made certain to maintain an impatient expression before the watchful eyes of the custodian.

"You don't have to call me back, Marty. Can you just answer 'yes' or 'no'?"

"Sure."

"Well 'yes' or 'no,' can you come visit me this afternoon."

"Yes, actually. I think I can do that."

She seemed to sigh with relief. "So, so good of you. I'm really glad. You just come any time. Or come several times. I'll be here. Waiting."

"Thank you. Talk to you soon." He pushed the "end call" button and put the phone back in his pocket. "Sorry for the interruption, Horace. So you are bound and determined to capture the pest yourself and you don't want to call in an exterminator."

"I'll get him, Pastor. Vermin don't belong in my church and I'm sure to be rid of him."

Larsen drew a deep breath. "I'd hate to be that rat, brother."

He parked in front of the complex in one of the two spaces reserved for Joan Celeste's apartment and went to the numeric pad alongside the glass front doors. Impatiently, excitedly, he tapped in the code Joan had shared with him five years before, explaining it was her birth date.

"It's easy to remember, Pastor," she had said. "September 8th. So just type in 0-9-0-8 and hit the star key."

He opened the door and started down the hallway that led to apartment 1D.

"Funny," he muttered. "So many things she told me about

25

herself, but she never said she had an exquisite daughter."

He stopped before the apartment door and knocked—firmly enough to be heard by someone expecting him, softly enough not to attract attention from the apartments up and down the hall. The door opened part way, only Ange's head visible to him.

"Hi." Her voice was sweet, welcoming. "Please come in."

She didn't open it much more as he squeezed through, stopped and turned to see she was completely naked. She leaned her back against the door to close it, engaged the deadbolt without taking her eyes off him and stood watching him. Her crimson nipples were erect.

He stared at her, wondering how long he could go without reaching out for her. "I like that outfit. It suits you. You look very . . . appealing."

"Thank you, Marty. I decided not to waste time with clothes."

He pressed himself against her and her against the door. He kissed her, as a long-thirsty soul drinks cool water. "You are so thoughtful."

"And anyway, my panties were getting wet waiting for you."

Ange sucked his tongue into her mouth and held it there as she began to undo his shirt. Her fingers, swift and unerring, ran across his bare chest, liberated his shirttail and dropped to his belt and zipper. His pants sagged to his knees and he felt her grasp his penis, half erect. It was only then she leaned her head back to breathe.

"Sorry I'm so forward," she said. "I hate being the only one who's aroused."

". . . You're not."

"Um hmm. So it seems. And not the only one who's wet." She kissed him again, gently. "Where shall we put this bad boy?"

"Oh. Well . . ."

They kissed again. She slipped his shirt off his shoulders and dropped it unceremoniously on the floor.

"Actually I do have a place in mind," he said.

She dropped to her knees and pulled off his shoes and socks and slipped his slacks and underwear off completely, so that he stood before her as unclothed as she was. Before she rose, she grasped his cock again and squeezed it, slowly sliding her hand toward her and milking a thick drop of pre-cum from it onto her index finger. Looking up at him, she slipped her finger into her mouth.

"That's Marty all right," she whispered. ". . . You want me?"

"Oh yes."

Ange stood and took his hand in hers. "Well, pretty boy, come to bed with me and fuck my silly brains right out."

It was, he thought, a strange procession: holding hands and walking slowly and silently through the living room into the bedroom and to the bed, his engorged member swinging from side to side with each step. He stopped and watched her put her knees on the bed, sit down with her back to the pillows and turn toward him with an expression of regal expectation. Like so many other moments in his time with Ange, there was nothing else in his experience to which he could compare this.

As he climbed onto the bed, she reached out and put her hands on either side of his chin. She pulled their faces together even as she slid down and eased him on top of her. Her legs wide, he could feel the hot wetness of her sex against his member. And, in case he couldn't, she rubbed the slick lips of her vagina against his erection. He was so aroused and she so wet that his glans slipped inside her with no guidance. Her hands on his lower back, she forced him down, the length of him inside her passage.

"Wait, wait, wait!" she whispered. She smiled at him, their faces scant inches apart. "Eat my pussy first, Marty."

He gazed into her warm chocolate eyes. "That sounds tasty."

As he slid his face down the length of her body, she arched her back and turned her head to the side in anticipation. Putting his hands beneath her buttocks, he lifted her bottom off the bed, the languid, saturated, purple labia just before him. He felt her tense, then relax as his mouth descended upon her vagina. She quivered as she sucked her clitoris against his teeth and teased it before forcing his tongue as far into her passage as it would go. With a thumb he caressed and pressed the clit while he sucked and pulled at her inner lips with his mouth.

Moments later, Ange's eventual moan seemed cautionary, as if she were warning him of something that was about to happen. "Oh, oh, pretty Marty. . . . Oh, oh."

"Oh, oh, what?"

It seemed then that a little seizure took her, her limbs shaking momentarily, relaxing, then shivering again. And the flavor of her effluence and the flow of it grew richer and thicker—almost bitter, potent, intoxicating.

"Creamy delight," he uttered quietly.

She lay still on the bed before him, her eyes closed for the better part of a minute. Then, placing an arm around his neck as she looked up at him again, she smiled.

"Act Two, my love," she said. ". . . Want me to suck him?"

"You do in I'll pop in ten seconds."

She giggled. "Then make him come inside me."

He felt her grasp the throbbing penis and guide it forward into her. Wet and supple as her sex was, she startled him by tightening her labia on his member. A girlish delight spread across her face.

"Wonder who can come first, Marty?"

"I'm pretty sure it's going to be me."

She raised her hips and lowered them, and took his hand and pressed it against one marvelous breast, the areola surrounded by a dozen tiny bumps, the nipple wooden. Slowly, gradually the pace of their intercourse quickened. As it did, she moved less and less, her head drooping to the side, her hands limp on the sheets.

"I . . . told you, Marty. . . . Fuck me, baby. . . . Fuck me."

She began to quiver once more. Even though he had not climaxed, the point of their union was awash in liqueur. Something within him held the orgasm at bay, something that did not yet want to relinquish the splendor and power of this moment to the coming relief and fulfillment.

"Ange . . ."

"Go ahead . . . love. . . . Fill me. . . . Come in me." She took a breath and wrapped her limbs, arms and legs, around him, pressing so tightly to him that his movement was restricted. "Come with me. . . . Now."

He let it go then, his body yoked indivisibly to hers in the lovers' knot. He found her lips and they kissed as the thrusting of his hips gradually ceased and ragged breathing took the place of the motion.

At the instant he woke, Larsen realized he had no idea how long they laid together, wrapped in each other.

His legs were over hers and she had covered them with a

sheet. Ange had been awake—perhaps the whole time—watching him.

"How long . . .?"

She gave him a different smile, womanly and serene. "Twenty minutes. Maybe thirty. Not long. Seems like you needed the rest."

Larsen rolled onto his back. "I fell asleep." He glanced at her. "I can't believe how unguarded I am with you."

"Yes. Really. . . . You know what I like? There was no hypocrisy today, was there? When I asked you to come over, I didn't have to make up any story about having things of Mother's for you to take to the church. And you didn't ask about it. You knew why you were coming over and I did too. No bones about it. . . . Well, one maybe. But that's why I could be at the door naked, because there was no deception or pretense that we needed in order to deceive ourselves about what we wanted and needed."

Basking in the odd glory of the moment with an unusual feeling of clarity and peace, he reflected on her words.

"So," he asked, "are you saying that I'm my truest self when I'm enjoying hot, adulterous sex with the daughter of a dead parishioner?"

"Oh! What a buzz kill you are, you big shit." She sat up and propped pillows behind her so she could lean back against the headboard. "How very natural it comes to you to let the air right out of our emotional intimacy."

Part of him wanted to ask if he were supposed to be having emotional intimacy with this gorgeous woman who was not his wife. Saying that would, he realized, completely destroy the moment. So he decided to make light of the situation.

"I think it's strangely funny," he said, "that a guy can be more open and relaxed with someone he doesn't know all that well than he can be with the people he's around every day." He sat up, leaning forward. "Why is that, counselor?"

She faced him. "Let's make a deal. A real deal. A deal to be real."

"What?"

"In this apartment, when we are together, for as long as we're together, it's the real thing. No posturing. No put on. In here we tell the truth—to ourselves and to each other. So in here I don't have to be a counselor and ask you how your mom potty trained

29

you. And you have to drop all that pretentious preacher bullshit."

He laughed. "'Pretentious preacher bullshit?' That's a new one. I never heard that before."

"I'm glad you think it's so funny. 'Cause my bet is that you can't pull it off. You've been 'Pastor Larsen' for so long that you can't just be 'Marty' anymore—if you ever were."

He stared at her unconcealed, unselfconscious nakedness as he considered her words. Was it totally cynical, or perhaps self-pitying, of him to say there was no longer a "Marty" who was not "Pastor Larsen," that in fact there might never have really been a "Marty." He decided against saying it. Even if she was not in counselor mode, she was going to call him on anything she thought was bullshit.

"Well, since we're being completely open honest," he said, "let me ask you about something you said, and you can give me a totally truthful answer."

"Shoot."

". . . You said, 'For as long as we're together.' I've been wanting to ask you how long that would be. How long will you stay before you go back to Florida?"

She shrugged and her breasts jiggled. "I'm not sure. A couple weeks probably." She studied his face. "Does that suit you?"

"It will have to, I guess." He tapped his fingers against the sheet, spotted by the emissions of their love. "I don't know if I could keep on with this for very long."

Ange nodded slowly. "Now that's the truth. That's what I'm talking about. And you don't know how long you can be my lover because . . . ?"

"Well for starters," he slumped back against the headboard, "as hot as it gets between us, I might just spontaneously combust. Apart from that, it's also distracting as hell."

"Distracting?"

"Yeah. I'd much rather be making love to you than calling on LOLs and LOMs."

"LOLs?"

"Little old ladies. And little old men. You see, when I'm here with you, my excuse is that I'm calling on my nursing home folks. They're used to seeing me once every couple months. For every hour I'm here, I'm missing three visits. So when I leave here after being with you, I feel bad not just for making love to someone who isn't my wife, but also because I'm skipping out on seeing my homebound parishioners."

She burst out laughing. Because his had been a solemn admission, tinged with guilt, her reaction surprised him.

"That's funny?"

She nodded vigorously. "Oh, fucking funny! Do you not realize how regimented your life is? You just admitted to me that people are supposed to know where you are at all times. And not just that you're supposed to be making regular, constant pastoral visits, but that they are supposed to be twenty minutes long and, if you don't adhere to that routine, you have to beat yourself up."

". . . Well, just fifteen minutes visits, actually. You have to build in some travel time. And the traffic around St. Louis is always abysmal. . . . That's not the only way you're distracting."

"Do tell."

"Yep. Last Sunday morning at the early service I got up to preach and all of the sudden I thought about how you sat on top of me as we were making love the first time. And the look on your face when you climaxed. It's kind of difficult to lead worship when you're sexually aroused."

"I see. Hard to preach when you're hard? Do you suppose that's why clergy have worn robes when they preach for centuries—so no one can see it when they get an erection?"

He laughed easily. "I never thought of that. It's as good as any explanation I ever heard. . . . But it's not that you're just distracting. I worry that people will find out about us."

"Oh. I see." She studied his face. "You worry about that a lot?"

"Yes, whenever I'm not with you and I start thinking about you—which is a lot—I worry about us getting caught. . . . When I'm with you, I don't think about it all. I'm incredibly relaxed." He rolled his head back and looked at the ceiling. "Both times I was with you before I thought, 'That was by-god fantastic, but I'm never going back again.'" He glanced at her. "Then you call and ask me to come over, and I can't wait to get here. I guess I'm just weak when it comes to you."

"I think you're brave. You have to be very brave to tell me that, to say you're conflicted. I think that's a very intimate thing to

31

do. . . . What if you're not weak at all? What if coming to see me is actually the real Marty breaking through and asserting himself?"

". . . You're joking. Right?"

She stared at him, apparently trying to decide how to respond. "So let me ask you, if your basic human needs were being met elsewhere, would you have ever made love to me?"

"Uh. Maybe. There's a difference, you know, between what we want and what we need. I mean, if we had never met and never made love, I probably wouldn't have died for lack of sex. So, I guess my needs are being met." When she didn't reply, he said, "Although I do have friends who have left the ministry and explained to me it was because they weren't getting their needs met. I don't necessarily think they were talking about their sexual needs."

"And when they said, 'I'm leaving the ministry because there's not enough in it for me,' you said to them. . ."

"Well I tried not to say anything. It's their lives, not mine. But I did think they were being selfish. After all, you know you're going into a life of sacrifice when you go into the ministry."

Ange leaned over to the nightstand on her side of the bed and produced an electronic cigarette. "So I have a question for you, Marty. As a pastor, when do you know that you've sacrificed enough?"

"What?"

She chuckled. "Well it's like you said a minute ago, you can talk with me at a deeper level than you can with anybody else— even the people you're closest too. That has to do with you being a pastor, right? So you've given up verbal intimacy. I'm pretty sure you don't have a lot of sexual intimacy. I'm guessing you've made sacrifices in just about every part of your life: how you dress, how you speak in public, what you've given up for your family. Maybe what you've made them give up. So how will you know when you've made enough sacrifices to make God happy?"

". . . No. I'm not making sacrifices in order to make God happy."

"If you're not trying to make God happy, what the fuck are you doing in the ministry?"

The question totally stunned him. He realized he was trying to think of an answer that would placate her, not satisfy himself. As for himself, he didn't want to answer the question. Somewhere in the depths of his awareness was the notion that, semantics aside, she had in that very moment unearthed a deep absurdity in his understanding of what it meant to be a pastor—of what almost every minister he knew understood about the ministry.

And when he couldn't answer, she said, "What if it makes God happy that we got together and rejoiced in one another's bodies, because it filled a real need each of us experienced that wasn't being met?" When he turned his head toward her, she said, "What if God sent me here so the two of us could be together—if only for a few days."

"I . . ."

She exhaled a cloud of vapor. "I had to add that part about 'for a few days,' because if I said I was staying, you'd immediately start asking yourself, Mr. Paranoid, if I was trying to steal you from you wife. Which I'm not."

"Look. Don't you expect that every clergyman who was lonely and maybe a little repressed—and, okay, horny—said the very same thing to the person he ended up in bed with?"

"Yeah, and you're saying they were in denial about their true motives."

"Yeah, I am."

"And what percentage of them got to that lonely, horny place at least in part because of the crazy life the church forced on them?"

"I don't think it was the church. I think it was their own assumptions about what it meant to be a pastor."

"Okay. Is that what happened to you?" She gave him a clever grin. "Oh, and don't most people in your church share those same assumptions about what a pastor should be?" She giggled. "I bet you have a lot of 'pastor police' among your flock, don't you?"

He laughed, his head rolling back. "Oh yes. Horace and Mitzi Mixon. To the world they look like the church's most faithful members. To me they are nosy, gossipy pests. And then there is the women's Day Circle. And there is the 'Pastor-Parish Relations Committee.' That's the group I'm supposed to go to if I have an issue. They have these regular semi-annual meetings and ask if I have any problems. Well my moderator, Larry Looper, is my biggest problem and he's on the committee. So what am I supposed to do if I really need to deal with issues?" Larsen's expression sobered and he gazed down at the bed.

Ange had been watching him and her head tilted to one side in curiosity. She gave a gravelly chuckle. "So, members of your congregation are really watching you and making your life miserable?"

". . . The chief enforcement officer of my 'Pastor Patrol' is actually not a member of my congregation at all. It's our bishop. A guy named Richard Johnson."

". . . And I take it you've had a run-in with the bishop?"

He shook his head. "No. I'm too smart for that. Crossing that jackass is pretty much career suicide. If he doesn't like you—and I mean, just 'like' you—he will blackball you."

"Hmm. And what does that mean?"

"Well let's say you want to move up in the world—you know, from a smaller church to a larger one. If you piss this guy off for any reason, he will absolutely prevent you from moving at all. . . . In some denominations, bishops have that kind of authority. They aren't supposed to in our polity. Johnson does because he abuses his authority. A friend of mine, another pastor in the synod, was under siege in his church from some malcontents who had gravitated to positions of authority. James asked the bishop for help several times—three or four—and got no response whatever, so he contacted the synod board. Long story short, he got the help he needed, but he also got on Johnson's shit list. He tried for several years to relocate to any other congregation. Johnson left him right there in clergy hell. Finally James just retired. At fifty-two. . . The most—I won't say 'ironic'—cruel, paradoxical part is that our protocol is for the bishop to show up and celebrate the retirement of clergy. There he was on Pete's last Sunday, standing up in the chancel and saying all these platitudes about the retirement of a worthy servant of God." He shook his head. "What a complete asshole." He sighed. "And the worst of it is, Sunday that dick is going to be in my congregation, addressing my people."

"You're retiring?"

He laughed. "Uh, maybe. If our little affair comes to light. But no, he's managed to royally screw up the annual synod assembly and he's strong-arming me to try to save his ass."

"I don't get it."

"So, as the bishop, Johnson has all the synod's congregations and all its clergy over a barrel. Bishops love to make theological pronouncements and act like they have some special importance. In reality the main thing they do is match up pastors and congregations. And most of them have very little training in personnel or counseling."

"Seriously?"

"Come on, Ange. If these guys had the kind of credentials you have, they'd be seeing patients and charging for it. If they had 'human resources' training, they'd be in private enterprise. Johnson, however, is the worst. He is very poorly organized. He has no delegation skills. Honestly? He's just the worst kind of dumb—the kind who thinks he's smart. He's a bully and a misogynist."

"Hmm. So how does a guy like that manage to keep his job as a bishop?"

Larsen sighed. "From a theoretical point of view, I'd say he's the living embodiment of the Peter Principle. You know what I'm talking about? Lawrence Peter wrote that people rise to their 'level of incompetence' and from that they neither rise nor fall. Well, Johnson has been the bishop of this synod for a dozen years. By now everybody in the denomination knows he's a chump. They're not going to elevate him to any kind of higher authority. And no church search committee is stupid enough to want him as pastor. We're stuck with this asshole." He shifted on the bed. "Nobody wants to deal with him. He's trying to bully my council into hosting the annual synod fall assembly because the first couple churches he asked turned him down. He's going to get up in worship Sunday and talk about St. Timothy's hosting it, and in doing so it will seem like I should have brought this up to the congregation last winter."

Ange set her vape on the nightstand and stretched. "Well, pretty Marty, I can't permanently get rid of the guy for you. But at least—" She put a hand alongside his face and caressed him. "—I can make you forget about him for a little while."

Chapter Four

Larsen was struck by the silence of the three women with him in the car as he drove toward St. Timothy's and Sunday worship. Mary-Martha was surfing Facebook on her Droid, reviewing posts, videos and links with the same critical expression she wore when grading test papers. Donna, sitting in the back seat on the passenger's side, was using his tablet computer as an e-book reader, completely engrossed in what was likely a tale of teenage vampire zombies. Glancing in his sun visor mirror, he could see Daphne behind him, ear buds firmly implanted, staring out the window at the unremarkable streets of Manchester.

"All right, ladies. Could I interrupt for a moment?"

None of them focused on him, but each glanced at least momentarily in his direction.

"Ah. Thank you for your kind attention. Donna and Daphne, you remember five years ago when we first came to this parish? . . . You remember the very first Sunday, when Daph knocked out the little Bitmann kid's tooth?"

"I didn't knock it out, Dad. He grabbed the toy I was playing with and stuck it in his mouth to irritate me. I yanked it out and out came his stupid tooth."

"For god's sake, Martin," Mary-Martha said, exasperated, "she was seven-years-old and it was a loose baby tooth."

"The kid had it coming," Larsen said. "That's not the issue. What I'm talking about is the rule we set up after that Sunday. Do you remember it? . . . Do you?"

"The 'prime directive'." Daphne rolled her eyes.

"Which was?" he persisted.

Donna looked over the top of the tablet. "The prime directive was: 'Don't embarrass Dad.' How could we forget?"

"Right. You remember. So here's the deal: the bishop is coming to church this morning."

"Duh." Donna feigned her stupidest possible expression. "Is that possibly why there is no early service and we're all riding to church school together?"

"For this Sunday only, we are reinstituting the prime directive—just because you never know when the bishop is within earshot."

"Is Karen coming?" Daphne asked.

"Who?"

"Geez, Dad. It's Mr. Johnson's daughter. She's my age. She was at that middle school youth rally in Jefferson City with me and Donna last fall."

"Oh," Larsen said. "Well, I wouldn't think so. Unless she knew you guys would be looking for her and asked her dad if she could come."

Mary-Martha looked over her shoulder at Daphne. "So is Karen nice? Did you enjoy her?"

"She's okay, I guess. At least she's not a dick like her dad."

Larsen's shoulders bunched and his hands tightened the steering wheel. "Where—I mean, Daph, that's the kind of thing I'm talking about. You can't say that around the bishop, even if you're not talking about him. And you didn't tell his daughter anything you've heard said about him by me or anyone in the church, did you?"

Donna's expressive face was a mask of disbelief. "Give us some credit, Dad. We're not that dumb."

He stared straight ahead, until he realized his wife was staring at him, the slightest grin playing on her lips. He turned to her.

"Yeah, Dad. Give those girls some credit," she repeated. "Daphne. You are not to use the word 'dick' again. Do you understand?"

"Yes, ma'am."

Larsen reflected on the possible ramifications of his two daughters—especially unabashed Daphne—consorting with Richard Johnson's daughter. For five-and-a-half years, despite the emotional distance between them, the pastor had managed to stay off the bishop's shit list. And now, with Johnson wanting special favors from him and the congregation, Larsen didn't want to be in the position of owing anything to his clerical superior.

"All that time your dad was a pastor," he said softly in Mary Martha's direction, "did he ever have to deal with a bishop he . . . you know."

Her eyes turned back to the screen of her mobile, Mary-

37

Martha said, "In forty-two years of pastoral ministry, Dad actually served under only three bishops."

". . . Wow."

"Bishop Weiner was great—just the sort of minister a bishop is supposed to be. But he was older when Dad came into the pastorate, maybe about sixty. So Dad only had him for a few years. The last bishop in the synod Dad served under was Bishop Jerbic. He was good. Very professional. The hard thing for Dad was being twenty years older than the bishop. And Jerbic was up-to-date, current on everything. I think that made Dad feel like he was a little behind the times." She sighed. "The one in the middle, Bishop Neumann, he was the joker in the deck. Dad was stuck with him for . . . must've been twenty years."

"Karl Neumann?"

"Oh yeah."

"Oh I've heard about him. His reputation transcends all synods. He was a legendary screw up."

"Yeah. Well, I remember Mom asking Dad how things were going every time he had to deal with Neumann. He would say, 'Well, Pris, you always have to take the good with the bad.'"

Larsen shook his head. "Twenty years. Sounds like a prison sentence for a major felony. I cannot imagine being stuck with Johnson for twenty years." He turned to Mary-Martha again. "Surely you father had some strategy that made it possible for him to work with a bishop who was a tool. Surely he didn't just suffer through all that time."

She shook her head. "Dad just didn't let it get to him, Martin. Why are you letting Rev. Johnson get to you?"

". . . You really like this place, do you? You want to spend the rest of your life—or the next fifteen years of it—here in West County? Would you one day like to, maybe, move up in the world?"

She stared at him, her face impassive. "What does that have to do with Bishop Johnson?"

Larsen gazed back at her, trying to determine if she were misunderstanding his dilemma or if she was unconcerned about it.

"Theoretically our churches get to choose their pastors," he said. "In reality nobody gets in here or out of here without the bishop signing off on it. And ultimately Johnson has the power and the willingness to shoot down any change a pastor wants to make."

She shrugged. "Isn't that what a bishop is supposed to do?"

"Mom, are we going to move?"

"No, Daph. We are not going to move. At all."

Mary-Martha turned back to her cell phone. Larsen stared ahead. A wave of loneliness and defeat washed through him.

Sitting at the back of the chancel in a regal wooden chair beside Larry Looper, the Moderator of St. Timothy's, and listening to the bishop drone on, Larsen could feel his allotted sermon time evaporating.

"I just need five minutes, Martin," Johnson had said as they stood in their regalia alongside the choir, preparing for the opening procession. "I'll be concise."

"That's fine, Bishop. Take all the time you need."

Larsen knew from experience not to let Johnson start speaking until the opening liturgy had been completed. As Pastor, Larsen could shrink his sermon or even eliminate it entirely; members would complain in equal degrees if the sermon were too lengthy or too brief. Failing to conduct the liturgy, however, was not an acceptable possibility—a truth Larsen knew very well and one to which Johnson had proven oblivious.

Once on a dare during a men's retreat Larsen had timed the bishop's prayer of blessing over the Holy Eucharist. The prayer—earnest and comprehensive and encyclopedic and deathly ponderous—had been seven minutes long. Johnson regularly demonstrated he was incapable of saying anything in five minutes or less. And, with a task as significant as convincing a congregation to host the annual synod fall fellowship, he would take at least fifteen minutes. That this was a monthly communion Sunday had already forced Larsen to condense his homily.

Now, the longer Johnson spoke, the shorter Larsen's available sermon time became. He wondered if the members realized what the bishop's intrusion did to the quality of his message, how it floundered when he had to delete parts of it arbitrarily on the spur of the moment. More than that, he wondered why he had been foolish enough to spend four hours creating a sermon that now would only be preached at one service and would be abbreviated to no more than five or six minutes—if Johnson ever did shut up and sit down.

Lazarus Barnhill

He had called Looper the day before and asked him, as the highest lay authority in the congregation, to wear a suit this Sunday and introduce the bishop. It had to be said for Larry that he loved the authority and decorum of the moderator's position, even if he was a mediocre congregational leader. And he had done a good job that morning of introducing someone who was already known to everyone present—apart from the young couple sitting on the lectern side at the back of the sanctuary. They were first time visitors. Larsen frowned. These two innocents were having to listen to the boring, pompous ramblings of the bishop—and, after him, a chopped up, abbreviated sermon. It meant, experience told him, the couple very likely would not return.

He gazed across the sanctuary at the faces of the faithful, struggling to stay awake. Looper touched his elbow with the edge of a rolled up worship bulletin and the pastor turned toward him. The moderator unrolled the bulletin just enough for Larsen to see when he had made three marks: the Roman numeral three. Now the pastor was the one trying to resist—not slumber, but laughter.

Minutes before, just at the end of the liturgy as the offering had been taken up and the congregation had risen to sing the doxology and Johnson gathered his notes to speak, Looper had leaned close to the pastor and whispered, "So how many times will he cry?"

Bishop Richard Johnson wept every time he preached. It was a tendency he brought with him when he came to the synod as bishop, and one that caused the lay members of the synod's congregations to think he was sincere and compassionate—at least the first time they saw him do it. Over the years his tendency to cry, or at least contort his face and attempt to hold back never-seen tears, had metastasized to the point that he had to fight back sobs when announcing the death of elderly ministers, budgetary shortfalls and pancake suppers. Johnson apparently did not realize that no one took his emotionalism seriously. Or perhaps he hoped that an even greater superfluity of faux weeping would demonstrate the genuineness of his spirituality. Instead it prompted cynical questions of the sort Looper had asked—that and concealed snickers.

"Now, I think I've about exhausted the time your Pastor graced me with this morning, sisters and brothers." He glanced at Larsen

40

and gave a comely smile, as if conveying humble gratitude. "So let me conclude my comments by lifting up what I think is one of the most important reports you will be hearing this fall at the assembly. As you know, our denomination leads all others in refugee resettlement. And I know—even though St. Timothy's hasn't yet hosted any immigrant families—that mission work is close to your hearts. Though you are not nearly the largest congregation in the synod, you are always near the top in your outreach giving—both by percentage per member and by actual dollar amount. Thus I know you will feel blessed when you hear . . ."

Doing his best to show no emotion beyond sincere interest, Larsen wondered if the bishop had any awareness that he had insulted him and the congregation multiple times. Johnson made it sound as if the pastor told him to take all the time he wanted. . . . Well, actually that was exactly what Larsen had done, but only a dunce would think it was acceptable to drone on for fifteen or twenty minutes in making an announcement that required sixty seconds at most.

Then too even Johnson had to know it was a point of contention between St. Timothy's and its pastor that the church would send disproportionate amounts of money to the denomination and synod for mission work—as long as they didn't have to engage in it personally. No mission trips. No hosting of refugee families. No direct hospitality for mission workers.

And why would he talk about size of the church? The congregation's membership, like most in the synod, had plateaued before Larsen arrived. One of the ironic aspects of calling Martin Luther Larsen was the avowed intention of the membership to hire a "younger pastor with a young family so as to attract young, growing families." Once Larsen accepted the job, of course, the congregation resisted all his efforts at evangelism—while still paying lip service to the need for growth. That the church membership had increased during Larsen's pastorate was a tribute to his dogged persistence at pursuing potential members, not any real effort on the part of the membership. The bishop, he thought, had an uncanny way of poking the church in all its sore, awkward places.

As Johnson droned on, Larsen found himself wondering if he would ever work with a really good bishop. Bishop Stewart, who had received him so graciously at the beginning of his seven year ministry in Dallas, had been wonderful. When Larsen came to interview with Concordia Church in person, Stewart had taken him to the art museum, and driven him past White Rock Lake and the North Park Mall. He had escorted him to his favorite restaurant on South Greenville Avenue, promising the best hamburger in Dallas—and delivering it. His hospitality, along with the real peace and wisdom he imparted, had emotionally prepared Larsen for the meeting with the contentious Concordia search committee and even made him willing to accept the call they extended. Stewart, however, had been an interim, an older, already retired minister called back into temporary service by the synod. Bishop Gustofson, who succeeded him—just in time to do Larsen's installation as pastor of Concordia—was someone who, in the words of his synod colleagues, lacked any "bedside manner."

It had been in Dallas that Larsen began to recognize the virtue of support from his clergy colleagues, both in and out of the denomination. Brother Rafe Miller, the Church of Christ preacher who sought him out—who called on the phone during his second week at the parish and asked if he could come by to introduce himself—had become his fast friend and true advisor. And it was Miller who helped him realize that, no matter how absurd and hypocritical his congregation and denomination were, Larsen was better off than so many ministers of other faiths.

Sitting in the little café on Garland Road one Monday morning, Larsen had asked Rafe how Sunday had been.

Casually, Rafe said, "Worship was okay. Had a couple new families visit. Met with the elders after church and talked them out of firing me again."

Larsen stopped stirring his coffee and stared at Rafe to see if he were joking. "You talked them out of firing you? Again? You mean they fired you before and you came back?"

"No, no. About once every two or three months they have an emergency meeting of the elders right after church—but never when the Dallas Cowboys have a noon kickoff. They ask me to explain why the church hasn't added any new members or why I said something in a sermon that sounded vaguely liberal or maybe ecumenical or not biblically literal. They never accept my explanation, whatever it is, and then say they're going to vote on whether or not to fire me."

". . . Oh my god."

"When they get to that point, I immediately tell them never again will I do whatever it was I did and ask them to give me another chance. So they postpone the vote and I'm good for another couple months."

"Well, what sort of awful things have you done that they want to fire you for?"

"Meeting with you, for one thing."

"What? Me?"

"Yeah. One of the 'deeply faithful' members of my church saw me eating with you here one morning. It was clear to them, with you wearing that backwards collar, that you're not Church of Christ. They reminded me that means you're going to hell." He looked up from toast he was slathering with strawberry jelly. "I been meaning to pass that on to you, by the way. Of course, living in Texas is ideal preparation for the eternal fires of damnation."

"Oh. . . . So is this supposed to be a secret now? Aren't you taking a big risk meeting with me?"

"Not at all. I told them that I'm making some good progress in getting you to leave your apostate religion and convert to the Church of Christ."

"Okay." He smiled broadly. "And what should I tell one of your parishioners when they call to ask me when I'm joining up with you?"

"Call you? Ha. Never happen. Most of them think they'll get churched just for talking to you."

"Churched?"

He wiggled a piece of bacon between his thumb and forefinger. "Don't y'all 'high church' folks know that means kicking people out of the fellowship."

"Oh. 'Excommunicate,' you mean."

"We don't use big words in the Church of Christ." He sipped his orange juice. "Big fancy theological words only serve to mask liberal ecumenism and a secret belief in universal salvation. One thing about us is that we aren't foggy on what we believe. We believe we have the truth. Actually it's more than believing. It's knowing. Beyond a shadow of a doubt. And if you have the right answer for every soul on earth, you don't want to consort with those who are wrong and damned. It might rub off on you. That's especially dangerous if you're a preacher. You might fall and then lead others away from the true faith." He nodded. "That's why they told me when I first came that, if tried to involve our church in fellowship with any other religious body, it was a sign I was deviating from the truth and I'd be fired on the spot."

He studied Rafe's face. "You're serious. Aren't you?"

"Oh yeah," he said solemnly. "You think I could make up bullshit like that?"

Larsen laughed. "So is that the real reason they want to fire you, because of that irreverent little attitude of yours?"

"Oh no. I would never speak this way to them. They never see this side of me. And honestly, they don't want to fire me. They just want me to think they'll fire me."

"Why?"

His head tipped to one side. "I guess it's like, when a homely girl snags a handsome guy who's a little bit of a weak person and a people-pleaser. She constantly points out his shortcomings and threatens to leave him. He responds by investing himself in making her happy so he won't lose her. And as long as she can get him to play along and pursue her, he won't realize what an insecure hound dog she is."

Larsen laughed out loud. "Well she sounds like a hound dog all right. So I guess you never say, 'Hey, are you guys not in touch with how lucky you are to have any pastor, let alone one who actually gives a shit'?" He leaned back in his chair. "I know how much you work Rafe. You call on every new visitor the day after they visit you church. Anybody in your church goes into the hospital, you visit them every day until they go home. You stay with people the whole time their family members are having surgery. . . . How can they not know how lucky they are? You are just slavishly devoted to them. . . Are they paying you so much money that you feel like you have to do whatever they ask?"

". . . They pay me $24,000 a year."

His mouth dropped open. "You are kidding me. You have three kids and a wife and you work sixty hours a week for $24,000?"

"Yeah. That was the source of our biggest disagreement. The one time I fought back."

"'Cause you wanted more money?'"

"No. I started selling insurance on the side to supplement my income. I wasn't selling it in the church, but folks found out. They pretty much always do. Sure enough the next Sunday they called me in and wanted to know why I was wasting my time selling insurance instead of building the church. I told that I was only selling insurance after I finished all my week's church work. And I told 'em I had a kid getting ready for college and you can't send a boy off to school when all you're making is a subsistence wage. They told me I should do a better job of managing the money God gave me. Then I got mad. I asked them if they thought they could do what I've managed to do with the little they give me. That stopped those guys cold, because they knew I know how much they're worth. They just adjourned the meeting right then— without saying they were going to fire me, without a closing prayer. I think they were afraid I was going to ask for a raise—and they'd rather I sell insurance than get a raise."

Larsen shook his head. "How long is their term? When do you get a new set of elders?"

"New elders? Dream on. Not in our polity. The church theoretically elects elders—but it mostly cronyism. And once you're an elder, you're an elder for life. That's the way it's always been with us. The elders run the church."

"Well can't you split them up—get more than half on your side so they stop their insane threatening to fire you."

"There are only three elders. The patriarch of the church, Mr. Downey, his brother-in-law Eldridge and his best friend Douglas. Eldridge and Douglas are always going to do whatever Downey tells them to do."

"They sound more like warlords than elders."

"If you don't like it, you can move on. Anyway that's what I was told as a kid. 'There are lots of churches out there you can go to, Rafe—all filled with people who are going to hell. If you don't want to be one of God's elect and go to heaven, you can always move on.'"

He stared at his friend silently. ". . . I guess, if you put up with that treatment and that ignorant grandiosity—and you don't move on, then you must really love your congregation and the ministry."

Miller nodded. "That's what a lot of us preachers tell

ourselves. My wife, on the other hand, tells me I'm a masochist. And a stupid one at that."

"Well," he stirred the cold remains of his coffee, "I just couldn't handle what they put you through." When Miller was silent for a moment, he glanced up at him. "What?"

"You need to not delude yourself, Martin. You endure the same stuff I do. It's just a matter of degree. We're all whores for our churches. I just happen to bend over farther and take it deeper than you do."

"Amen!"

It was Richard Johnson's voice, breaking his reverie. The bishop had apparently finished his diatribe, to a smattering of applause from the 150 worshippers. He nodded to the congregation and then to Larsen—as if the pastor had asked him to drone on and on and he had fulfilled his obligation. He picked up his notes and walked to the tall chair on the far side of the chancel.

As Larsen allowed the bishop to make his flourishes and settle his cassock into his seat, he considered how he would respond to what had been said. It would be a slap at the bishop if he said nothing. If he parroted the bishop's lengthy request to host the fall fellowship, it would make Johnson seem weak and needy—a sort of mocking diminishment of the eighteen minutes the congregation had just endured. While he needed to acknowledge and support the bishop's speech, he also wanted in some way to let his members know the synod's request had suddenly come upon them—that he had not failed or procrastinated in asking permission of St. Timothy's to host the assembly.

He rose and stepped to the pulpit, opening the Bible Johnson had closed and spreading the sermon notes. Looking across the sanctuary, he tilted his head slightly to the side and began.

"On behalf of the entire membership of St. Timothy's, Bishop, we express our appreciation to you for sharing with us in worship this Sunday." He glanced at Johnson. "This was a win-win situation for us. Not only did we get to hear of the work of our synod and receive your invitation to participate in it by hosting the fall assembly, but now we get to have a really short sermon."

There was a titter of courtesy laughter from the pews. Larsen's expression grew earnest as he continued.

"Now our bishop is too gracious to ever point this out, but he

46

is here today to ask us to host the fall synod assembly because a sister congregation of ours was unable to fulfill that role. I am flattered that, this late in the church year, when other congregations were not able to extend hospitality to the entire synod, our bishop turned to us. One of the things I learned years ago when I first became a pastor is that our churches and our synods and our denominations will only succeed if their leaders succeed. Bishop Johnson—Christ's servant, our friend—has come to ask our support, come to ask us to share our rather legendary hospitality. The decision, of course, resides with the council. I certainly hope and will encourage the council at our meeting today to respond affirmatively that we might host all our sister congregations this fall. . . . And now, before the sermon disappears completely, let us meditate upon the Gospel and its lesson for us today."

Chapter Five

He pulled the sheet up to his chest as he listened to her moving about in the kitchen. The refrigerator door opened, followed by the sound of a soft drink can being opened and a drawer sliding.

Larsen stretched, recalling the abrupt way she had turned away from him after a final kiss and hopped childlike from the bed. He had watched the rhythmic swing of her magnificent behind disappear through the bedroom door. A tranquil curiosity descended upon him. What was she doing in the kitchen?

Ange appeared through the door again, carrying a full tumbler in one hand and an open jar in the other. She slipped back onto the bed beside him, somehow managing to cross her legs and sit facing him, unselfconscious about her nakedness, the petals of her labia slick with the flow of their love.

"I brought something for you." She held the fat, short jar beneath his chin. "Maraschino cherries. I thought I'd give you some of these—since you didn't get mine, you poor thing. And here's a little soda to whet your whistle."

He laughed.

"I know you like sweet red cherries."

Larsen frowned. "How would you know that?"

"Mom told me, of course."

"Really? And how did she know that?"

She set the glass on the nightstand and produced an olive fork. Stabbing a cherry, she held it to his lips and smiled, mouth open, as he took it between his teeth.

"Banana splits. She said you liked extra cherries on your banana splits."

"Oh yeah." He swallowed. "We had a youth fund raiser. The kids made banana splits to earn money for their ski trip. The old fart going through the line in front of me said he didn't like cherries. So I said to add his onto mine." He chuckled. "They must've put a dozen cherries on it."

She popped a cherry into her mouth and sucked hard before chewing it. "I have a question for you."

"Yeah?"

"Yeah. What was that look you gave me when you came through the front door?"

"Oh. . . . Well. You had your clothes on."

"Yeah?"

He shrugged. "The last time I came over you were naked when I came in."

Ange laughed. "Did my wearing clothes today present an unacceptable degree of difficulty for you?"

"No. Nothing like that." He swallowed the next cherry she held up to him. "In fact your clothes came off very nicely. And it was fun taking them off. I just thought, well, maybe we weren't going to make love today. Like, since you were still dressed, maybe it was your time of the month."

"Oh. No. Not anymore. I don't have that issue, so to speak. Isn't that what they called it in the Bible—an 'issue'?"

"I see. Well you're too young for menopause, I'm guessing. . . . So did you have a hysterectomy, if you don't mind my asking?"

"I don't mind. Yes. Vaginal. No scars. No uterus. Got the ovaries still though."

"Have kids?"

"No."

". . . Were you ever married?"

"Nope, Pastor. I never was."

"Well—and I know this is none of my business—how did you avoid that?"

She shook her head. "Nobody ever asked."

Larsen stared at her. "That's a little hard to believe, Ange. Let me guess. All your psychological training convinced you men are universally screwed up, so you decided never to marry one."

"Honestly, Marty," she said slowly, "no one ever asked."

For a minute he did not respond, gazing at her. "You're going to have to explain that one to me."

"Ha. I hardly know you."

He laughed. "You can trust me. I'm a pastor. I'll keep your secrets."

Her expression was both coy and candid. "It's simple, Marty. I'm too honest. I don't hold back on anything. I think, as a general rule, nobody wants to live a lifetime with that level of truthfulness."

"I see. So—let me guess—when you've gotten close to someone—"

"I never said I got close to anybody, Marty."

"Haven't you?"

". . . What would you say if I said I've never been emotionally closer to another human being than I am to you?"

"I'd say you aren't as honest as you let on."

She laughed, unabashed. "My turn, Pastor. Speaking of how you dress, why don't you ever wear your clerical collar when you come to see me? Is it more acceptable for a minister to have an affair if he's not in uniform?"

"For your information, I hardly ever wear a clerical collar—even when I'm not on my way to have sex with a deliciously beautiful woman."

"You were wearing it when we met at the funeral home."

"Yes. I pretty much just wear it on Sunday morning and for those occasions when I need the advantage it gives me. Like when I go to hospice or a nursing home or the hospital, nurses give me less shit about going in to see my really sick parishioners when they see the collar."

"Ministers get special privileges?"

"Some do," he said. "Most liturgical clergy—high church guys like me—have to have some pastoral counseling training before they get ordained. So when they see the collar, nurses and administrators sort of understand we're not totally going to fuck up and say the wrong thing."

"I thought only a doctor could say the wrong thing in an ICU."

"Ha." He shook his head. "One time I was standing with a young woman—she was probably thirty or so—beside her husband's bed. The guy was suffering with encephalitis. His brain was swollen up and he was in a coma, right? Supposedly he couldn't hear or speak. Only you have to know patients really can hear what's being said around them. So his wife is talking and she says, 'Yeah, I know he might die.' All the sudden this guy starts writhing. Good thing he was restrained. He would've come off that bed and yanked out every tube and hose they had stuck in him. And she kept right on talking, so caught up in her own emotions that she was totally oblivious to his reaction. So I lean over close to his ear and say, 'Of course we know, Audrey, that Kurt is not

going to die. We're going to pray and demand that God heal him.'
I just started praying and kept on praying. Within a few seconds he
started to relax. Pretty soon he was still again."

"Maybe he was dead."

Larsen laughed out loud. "No! He lived. Just like I said."

"So your prayer was answered?"

"No, I'm not saying that."

"Doesn't God listen to clergy prayers more than everybody
else's? Don't you pretty much always get what you pray for?"

He gave her a skeptical smile. "Now think—what would
happen if all us ministers got our prayers answered?"

"It would be a better world?"

"Oh hell no. No even any better than it is right now. Preachers
are pathetically idealistic. The Almighty is smart enough not to
answer all our prayers."

She thought about his words. "Well don't all preachers learn
what to pray for and what not to pray for in preacher school?"

"Not all preachers go to seminary. And not all divinity schools
teach the shit that pastors really need to know—like what not to
say to people in crisis and not to let your 'pure theological
idealism' afflict other human beings."

"I see. And at your seminary you did learn those things. So if
the collar is a giveaway that you're the 'real deal' as a minister,
why don't you wear it all the time?"

He opened his mouth wide to accept another cherry, chewed and
swallowed it. "I remember when I first got ordained. I couldn't wait
to wear the collar. That way everyone knew I was a pastor."

"And you quit wearing it because . . . ?"

He sighed. "Because when you wear it everyone knows you're
a pastor."

"That's not what you want anymore?"

". . . It gets real old real quick. Wear that collar around for a
while and you walk right into people's assumptions about how a
minister is supposed to act and talk and believe." He opened his
mouth, accepting another cherry, chewing and swallowing it
before he continued. "Not long after I was ordained I went to a
barbershop to get a haircut. I was pretty new in town and I didn't
have regular barber yet. I sat down in the chair with this girl who
was a few years younger than me. She starts cutting my hair and

51

we start talking. It was just a casual conversation. I don't even remember what we were talking about.

"Five or six minutes into the cut, she happened to ask me what I did for a living. I told her I was an ordained minister." He shook his head. "She clammed up completely. I was watching her face in the mirror, right? You could see how stressed out she got. Suddenly she has no idea what to say. She's clipping my hair at super speed. I'm praying she doesn't cut off the top of my ear." He smiled at Ange's giggle. "She could not finish my haircut quick enough. As she took my money, she avoided any eye contact. . . . I walked out the door and said to myself, 'And I wasn't even wearing my collar.'"

She grinned slyly. "I thought all you holy men wanted to be treated differently than ordinary folks."

"I don't know if I ever did want deferential treatment, but I sure don't now. I just want to be a human being again instead of whatever it is people think ministers are. Most times I just hate that damn collar."

"Maybe you should've signed up for one of those denominations that don't wear collars."

"Yeah well, a lot of those poor dumb bastards go out of their way to make themselves stand out and look like preachers, don't they? They're always 'suited up' and clean shaven and carrying some little Bible or prayer book and wearing a cross. And then there is the Pentecostal hairdo."

"The what?"

"'Pentecostal hairdo'," Larsen said. "Haven't you ever seen some guy dressed to the nines with his hair grown long, teased up and swept back?"

". . . Well, yeah, I guess so."

"That's the 'Pentecostal do.' It's amazing the way guys dress so as to say to the world, 'Hey, I'm a fucking minister!'"

"Oh, now, Marty, they're not all like you."

He bent forward, laughing. "Well, here's the thing. It holds for the collar, the cross, carrying the Bible and wearing ridiculous clothes and the televangelist hairdo. I want people to know I'm a Christian not because of what I'm wearing but by how I act."

She stared at him, waiting for the weight of his hypocrisy to bow him down.

"Well, okay," he responded, "how I act when I'm not naked with you."

"So people treat you differently when they find out you're a minister," she said. "Does that bother anybody besides you?"

"Besides me?"

"You know, like your wife and kids?"

He shook his head. "No."

"Really? You're sure of that? I don't see how it could not bother them?"

"No, actually I am sure. I was ordained before either of the girls were born. They've never known anything other than being the 'pastor's kids.' And Mary-Martha's father was a pastor for forty years. This crazy shit existence feels natural to her."

"So is that why she married you, 'cause she enjoyed the minister's lifestyle?"

Larsen toyed with the edge of the pillow behind his head. "That's a damn good question, actually. I guess there were times, after we'd been married a few years, when I came to believe she married me because I was going to be a pastor, and not because she loved me."

Ange squished a cherry behind her teeth. "I've counseled more than one spouse who wanted out when the man—or woman—they married decided on the ministry as a second career. It sounds like kind of the opposite with Mary-Martha. Would she have married you if you weren't going to be a pastor?"

"Hmm." He gazed down at the rumpled sheet spread over him. ". . . I think that's one of those questions that linger at the back of your mind you try never to ask yourself."

"Oh, you mean like, how much of the Bible is literally true?"

"Ha. Actually that's easier for me than wondering whether or not Mary-Martha really loved me."

"'Loved'? Not, 'loves'?"

"Oh, I think she loves me now. We've built a life together. We depend on each other. We're invested in each other."

"But she didn't love you before?"

He sighed, his head slumping to one side. "My older brother is Wendell Stuart Larsen, Jr. He grew up knowing he wanted to be an engineer, just like our father. And he is an engineer—a good one. My name is Martin Luther Larsen. My mother chose that name. As

53

you might guess, she's really big into church. She was giving me the most important name she could think of. From the earliest time I can remember, everyone in and out of our family assumed I was going to be a pastor. Everybody just understood that. By the time I was a junior or senior in high school, I understood it. "

"You never questioned the role your mom hung on you?"

"Not really. . . . Mary-Martha's dad was my pastor when I was in high school. I was fairly articulate as a kid, so he started including me as a worship leader. When Lent and Advent rolled around and somebody was needed to read passages of scripture or recite prayers or liturgy, I was always the 'go to.' It was assumed by everyone in the church and my family that I was headed to the ministry. So when I said, about Easter of my senior year, that I was going to college and then divinity school, it was like 'manifest destiny.' Nobody was surprised."

She smiled at him. "And was it always assumed you would hook up with Mary-Martha and marry her?"

A low, slow chuckle came from his chest. "Maybe so. We had dated off and on from the time we were sophomores. We weren't dating at the time I made the announcement that I was going to be a pastor. Right after that she calls me up and tells me she's free Friday night and I should take her to some chick flick that had just come out." He shook his head. "Just floored me. So I took her to the movie and then for frozen yogurt after that. We're sitting in the front seat of my mom's car at the yogurt place and she scoots onto the center console and leans against me—just presses her tits right against me. Now I should say she was not the sort of girl anybody ever got to second base with, right? And now she's rubbing herself against me. And she says in this deep, husky voice I never heard before—and haven't heard since, 'Martin, I've been saving myself for you since ninth grade.'"

Ange giggled and coughed.

"Yeah." He shrugged. "I guess we pretty much went steady after that. We didn't get engaged until I was a junior in college. Honestly, I didn't see the point in getting engaged. Everybody knew we were a pair."

"So after the yogurt night, she was hot for you?"

"'Hot for me?' Well not really. I think she was trying to tell me there was some underlying passion there that I was going to get

54

to tap into somewhere down the line. It sure wasn't right then. We did finally make love after we got engaged. Mary-Martha has never been particularly . . . I'm not sure exactly how to say it."

"Horny?"

He laughed. "Okay. Well, that does pretty well say it."

"And you were her first?"

". . . Yes, actually I was."

"But she wasn't your first."

"Uh, no."

Her head dipped to one side. "Well if you dated each other exclusively all those years, how did that happen?"

He shrugged. "We went to different colleges, a couple hundred miles apart."

Ange leaned back, stretching her bare legs and putting them over his. "So tell me about your first time."

"Your mom didn't tell you about it?"

They laughed together.

"Well Mom didn't know just everything about you. Some things I have to find out for myself."

"Why are you so interested?"

The muffled strains of "A Mighty Fortress Is Our God" sounded from the floor on his side of the bed. Larsen leaned over the edge and retrieved his cell phone from his pants pocket. The church's phone number lit the little screen.

"Oh shit. This is the church secretary."

"Okay," Ange replied. "Maybe I won't make any noise."

He grinned as he held the phone to his ear. "Hello."

"Pastor Larsen, this is Edith at the church."

"Yes ma'am. What can I do for you?"

"The bishop just called."

"Oh. To thank us for hosting the fall assembly?"

Edith thought about his question. "He might have said 'thank you.' Actually his reason for calling was to give us the menu he wants the women's group to serve at the assembly supper."

A stab of indignation passed through him. "And did you tell the bishop that beggars can't be choosers?"

Edith snickered. "I did not, Pastor. But I can call him back and tell him if you want."

"I'll tell him the next time I see him. What does he want served?"

55

"He says he's tired of chicken breasts, green beans, mashed potatoes and dinner rolls. We've had that three out of the last four assemblies. Instead he wants rib eyes, baked potatoes, corn cobs and broccoli."

". . . The bishop wants us to serve 200 steaks at the fall assembly?"

"Well, he said the buy-in would be expensive, but that St. Andrew would recoup its money from the participants."

He felt his jaw drop. "Excuse me, Edith, but aren't we locked in at a maximum of $10 a head for registration."

"Yes, sir."

"And the synod gets half of it?"

"Yes. To cover the synod's expenses."

"So we're supposed to serve steak, baked potatoes and roasting ears, tea and coffee for $5 a person for 200 people? And that's before dessert."

"I think he expects the women to provide homemade dessert."

He drew a deep breath. "Edith, every congregation knows it's going to lose money when it hosts the synod assembly. But if we serve what the bishop wants, we will go several hundred dollars in the hole."

When he didn't continue, she asked, "Do you want me to call Darlene—"

"I'll call her, Edith. And I'm telling you now in case it comes up, that the women can serve any sumptuous feast they can put together for $5 a head."

"Well what if the bishop—"

"I'll tell him any expense we incur that's not paid for by our half of the registration fees has to come out of our annual synod offering. It's rib eyes or his salary. That'll shut him up."

". . . It's your call, Pastor. Just don't forget to—"

"I'll call Darlene and have her pass it along to the ladies when I get back to the church."

There was a momentary pause as Edith reflected on his words. He could almost feel her curiosity swell.

"Where are you, Pastor?"

He cleared his throat. "I was headed to hospice to see Jewel and her family. Only I had to stop to get myself—" He exchanged glances with Ange. "—a cherry cream soda. As soon as I get through over there I'll head back. ". . . Anything you need while I'm in the city?"

"No, Pastor."

"Okay, thanks. See you soon, Edith." He pressed the red button that ended the call and waited until his home screen appeared.

"Yep, you really don't care much for your bishop."

"Uh, no."

"And it sounds like you don't like your secretary that much Better."

He shook his head. "She isn't my secretary. I inherited her. And whoever follows me will inherit her as well. And I can assure you, if I had said anything really damning about the bishop, she'd already be on the phone to tell him."

"So she's a gossip and tattletale—"

"And the St. Louis County citizen voted most likely to throw the pastor under the bus."

"And she and the bishop are tight, I take it."

Larsen sighed. "The dynamic is this: Edith sucks up to the ultimate authority in any given situation. Our denomination is famous for allegedly having 'strong pastor' polity—meaning what the pastor wants, the pastor gets. In reality that's a myth perpetuated by people who want a reason to complain about whatever it is the pastor wants. 'The pastor shouldn't get his way just because he's the pastor.' However in the synod, which is the fellowship of all the churches of our denomination in this area, the highest authority is the bishop. Edith will kiss his ass anytime he's around to bend over. If Johnson got run over by a commuter train tomorrow, I'd be Edith's new best friend. Until we got a new bishop." He sighed. "Of course, just about any new bishop we get is better than the one we got."

She cocked her head. "Even after he came to your church just to worship with you, you still don't like him?"

"Richard Johnson is pretty much a dunce. The reality is, I don't know a soul in the synod who thinks he's competent—let alone doing a good job."

"Yeah, you told me all about him. He wrecks people's careers. So do you think he's just snarky and pissy? Or is he out-and-out evil?"

Larsen stopped, reflecting on her words. "My god. What a good question. How smart do you have to be to be evil? Most of the people I would call 'evil' have been pretty bright. You know, serial killers. Dictators. But stupid people can do really bad things too."

She nodded. "We call them 'Congress.'"

He chuckled, his chin dropping forward. "Johnson is almost enough of a nincompoop to be a congressman. Maybe we could get him to run. Otherwise we'll never get rid of him. He's entrenched. He's the ecclesial version of herpes and toenail fungus. But, honestly, he's not bright enough to be truly evil. . . . Now, on the other hand, I have encountered real evil in the church."

"Do tell."

"Yeah." He stretched. He pursed his lips. "You probably don't want to hear—"

"Oh I love morality tales," she replied quickly. "Since I have none, hearing about morals fills a void in my psyche. Go on. Tell me."

". . . Okay. It was like my first real test as a clergyman." He glanced at her. "In our polity, after you finish your seminary career, you have to do a one-year internship in a church before you can be ordained."

"Yeah?"

"I went to seminary in Denver and, surprise-surprise, when I was about to graduate I was contacted by a congregation in Kansas City that wanted me to come spend my intern year with them. Really I was stunned. It was an honor to be approached by these folks. It was a large church. Our denomination tends to be mostly small and middle sized churches, you know? So for this big dog to seek me out was . . . a really impressive deal.

"As it turned out, the person who pushed the selection committee to come after me was the pastor. A guy named Larkin." He grinned. "He kept making a thing out of that. 'What a team we're going to be: Larkin and Larsen.' . . . Now Mr. Larkin did not come from our denomination originally. He was from—I don't know—I think UCC?"

"I don't know what that is."

"Congregationalists—you know, like the Pilgrims."

"Oh."

"And years ago they joined with an old German group called the E-and-R and became the United Church of Christ. There are a fair number of them around here."

"Yeah."

"But Larkin left that fellowship and joined ours. He said he found the UCC to be too liberal and not biblical based."

"So it was a compliment to your team."

"Well . . . I never quite bought it. Lots of folks in that KC church, particularly a lot of the young leadership types, thought he was the 'second coming.' And he was always very solicitous with me. But there was something about him."

". . . Like?"

"He always spoke with that smarmy, pseudo-sweet Evangelical voice."

"What?"

"I don't know if you've ever listened to Evangelicals much—"

"What are Evangelicals?"

"They are the largest, most rapidly growing group of American, non-Catholic Christians. They tend to be fundamental in biblical interpretation, very conservative in their beliefs and very mechanical in their faith."

"I don't know what any of that means."

"It means that they believe the Bible is literally true, that they're very politically active and vote for the most conservative candidate, and that they believe they have the formula for keeping Jesus happy and getting exactly whatever they want in this life."

Ange rocked back on the bed. "Oh, I see. I got it. And this Larkin was one of them?"

"Theoretically he had no connection with them, but from the beginning I realized he had all the mannerisms of an Evangelical preacher. Whenever they talk, they always sound like they've been gargling molasses. So many of them talk with this phony sweetness. I guess it's supposed to pass for this abiding, gooshy attitude of accepting love they pretend to have." He raised an index finger. "But here is the real giveaway: Evangelicals cannot pray without using the word 'just.'"

"'Just'?"

He closed his eyes and assumed a faux smile and the sort of

tone he used to persuade his girls to go to sleep when they were tiny. "'Oh Lord Jesus, we just come to you today asking for your blessing. We just ask for our daily bread and whatever blessings you might bestow upon us that we might be strengthened just to do your work. We just pray for righteousness to prevail in our land that the good Christian men who founded our nation to make a safe haven for those of who come after to worship and praise you and just serve you with the abilities you have graced us with'—" Her laughter stopped him.

"So," she asked, "what's so evil about having a closet Evangelical for a pastor. Sounds like those guys are cocked and primed for big churches anyway."

"Yeah, well. It remains to be seen how many of those Evangelical megachurches will last for any length of time. The congregation I serve now is 115-years-old. In my opinion, megachurches are actually giant monuments built to enshrine the gargantuan egos of grandiose preachers."

"So," she asked, "what happened in the Kansas City church?"

His jaw tightened and his voice grew reflective. "Lots of times an ambitious preacher will take an existing church and break away from a denomination—not only ours, but just about any well-organized denomination that has a real polity. That way there are no rules or checks on their behavior except from the congregation itself—and the members of the church think these jokers are anointed."

"So Larkin tried to lead the Kansas City church away?"

He nodded. "Lead it? He tried to steal it. And he tried to enlist me to help him. Over the six or seven months I had been there, Larkin had mentored me and held me up to the congregation as potentially a good associate minister. I was good at starting new programs, good at pastoral care, good in the pulpit when he had me preach. I kept saying, when people said they would be sorry to lose me after my internship, that I was supposed to be a learner and that I was only going to be there for a year."

"Yeah?"

"I think he thought that, if he could butter me up and make me feel like I was following God's will, I'd go along with any plan he had to break the congregation free from the denomination. In a way, I wasn't all that surprised when he came slithering up to me

60

just around the end of the church year. A new council—that's the governing body inside the church—was about to be elected and Larkin talked about how our denomination had moved away from right biblical theology and that the church members were counting on us to lead them in the true paths of righteousness and the only way to do that was to sever our ties with the synod and go out on our own."

"I see. So you told him to fly a kite?"

"No. I asked him for a little while to think it over. After all, I told him, it meant I'd lose my standing in my denomination and I wouldn't get ordained. He said for me to take my time and to remember that there is 'man's ordination and then there's God's ordination.' I didn't want him to know how I really felt." He gazed at her. "You see, he made the mistake of hinting at his whole plan with me. After installing the new council—which would have been two-thirds made up of people he had handpicked, he was going to call a congregational meeting to propose a split from the synod. He said he was 'pretty sure' he had the support of the council and that he was sure the congregational vote would turn out in the proper way. . . . I knew what he meant. He had been packing the leadership with folks who would have followed him off a cliff. And it wasn't hard for me to figure out that, for several years, he had intentionally been bringing in ringers—'missionaries' from other Evangelical churches who were joining the church intentionally to vote for the split, with the promise that the church would be Evangelical afterwards. . . ."

"Wow. That is kind of evil."

He shrugged. "Theoretically, I suppose, the membership of a congregation can decide to go off in a different direction than the one it emerged from. That's how our movement came into being 500 years ago. But Larkin was trying to steal the church through infiltration. He was like a lot of preachers in the news these days: a lot more interested in their own aggrandizement than the welfare of the church they serve, or God's people who are in it."

"So what did you do?"

"I went to the bishop," he said. "Not alone. I took a few of the old time leaders with me, some men and women who had deep ties to the denomination and synod. Longtime members of the church I had gotten to know in the time I'd been at the church. . . . Whew. I still get worked up thinking about it. I quietly made an appointment with the bishop for the next Saturday morning and then I went around to see these folks. I said, 'You can keep a secret, right?' They knew something was up—and I know it made them anxious—but I didn't tell them anything. I just said, 'Saturday morning, be at the bishop's office. And don't tell another soul.' There was six of them and they all showed up."

"Wow. I take it none of them wanted to split and become Evangelical."

"Uh, no. . . . We had a wonderful, wise bishop in that synod. He and the others just listened as I spelled out Larkin's little scheme."

"And the Navy came riding in to chase off the pirates?"

"Well, it wasn't quite that simple. The way Larkin had things set up, if the typical progression of events had happened, he would have won. His group would have gotten the facility and changed the church to something that would have been completely unpalatable to anybody in our denomination."

"So what did you do?"

He smiled. "That group of folks who went to see the bishop had been leaders in the church for decades. They knew the church order inside and out. They sat there and planned a special called meeting of the council—the old council that was still in office, the one that wasn't packed with ringers. As cunning as Larkin was, they were way ahead of him. They voted down the report of the nominating committee and pushed back the annual meeting. The bishop called Larkin in and told him that an official synod inquiry was to be impaneled to investigate his conduct. So Larkin took two weeks of vacation and never came back. He ended up pastoring a new church start right there in town with a couple dozen families from the church."

". . . So, were you the hero?"

"Well . . ." His head dipped to the side. "Not really. I was told I could not talk about this to anyone. Because Larkin resigned the pastorate and retired his ordination in our denomination, there was no reason for a formal inquiry. So if we had gone around telling everybody who asked what he had done, he could have brought a suit against us. The bishop and church leaders told me I couldn't breathe a word of what happened to anyone. It was really strange—people asking me all these questions and I had to say, 'Gee, I'm in the dark too.'"

Ange chuckled softly. "So the hero got no reward for saving the church."

"Not officially. But I sure did get treated like a prince for the remainder of my time there. Seems like a lot of people knew I had done something good for the church—and that Larkin was a culprit."

"Why didn't they ask you to stay and be their pastor?"

"Oh, Lord! I was too young. The church was too big. I wasn't ready for it. I was just an intern." He nodded. "Still, there were sweet people who did everything to try to get me to stay—although I didn't really want to stay at the 'scene of the crime,' so to speak. It does something to you, to be involved in a plot like that, I mean. Sort of gives you a dirty feeling, like you need to get baptized again, even if you did what you did for the right reasons and the upright side prevailed. You still feel . . . slimy."

As the silence that ensued lengthened and he watched her stare at him, he began to wonder what she thought of him. Did she find him as manipulative and underhanded as the minister he had foiled? Had she thought him more graceful and spiritual than he had just demonstrated himself to be?

". . . Speaking of staying too long, I guess I'd better get dressed and head over to hospice."

She wiggled her eyebrows up and down. She smiled and he could not resist smiling as well.

"Got time for one last cherry?"

"Huh. Sure."

Ange tilted the jar toward herself and dipped her fingers into the juice, producing a brilliant, shining cherry that she held by the stem. For an instant she lifted it to his lips and, when he leaned forward to take it, she pulled it back and held it out of his reach. Her mouth open, she touched the cherry to one of her areolas, rolling it around and around the nipple—that suddenly seemed to protrude. Larsen leaned forward gently and closed his mouth around the dark circle, tasting the cherry juice and feeling her thicken in response.

Ange put her hand on his forehead and forced him back. He watched as she wiggled the cherry before him and ran it down her belly, incrementally moving slower and slower until the bright red rested against the maroon and pink of her clitoris. Ange set the cherry jar on the telephone table beside the bed and widened her legs.

"You could get eaten and fucked doing that."

"Promises, promises."

Larsen slid down flat on the bed, pulling her toward him and lowering her crotch to his chin. The flavors of the sweet cherry and the salty nectar of her vagina mingled maddeningly in his mouth. He felt his cock tighten and straighten almost instantaneously as she pressed forward, her weight on his face, her thighs against his ears. She massaged his scalp as he ate her, putting his hands on her buttocks and pressing her to him. After only a couple minutes, a jerkiness seemed to invade her limbs, as if she could not decide whether to pull herself even closer to him, or push him away. Then she stopped moving altogether and arched her back and the flavor of her depth took on a rich ripeness, irresistibly arousing.

She looked down at him with a serene benevolence. "Want to fuck me now, Marty?"

Ange scooted down his body, languorously, so that he did not know whether to pay attention to her breasts running hot across his face and chest or the effluent vagina making its way to his member. And when their sex came together, her labia encircled and accepted his engorged penis without guidance or hesitation. They joined rhythmically in perfect stately coupling, uninterrupted as he raised her chest enough to suck a breast into his mouth. It seemed to him they could go on in this way for hours, and he was content to let creation roll on without him so long as he could remain in this euphoria. And then she began to moan and quiver again, closing her eyes as the inevitable orgasm approached. The proximity of her climax roused him and he, pressing down on her behind with his hands, began to pound upward, to arch his neck.

"Marty . . ."

". . . Ange . . . I have to . . ."

"Come in me, baby. . . . Now. . . . Now."

And he did. It burst forth from him wildly and he clenched his teeth so he did not cry out. As for the woman, she drifted down onto him, sighing, spent.

Their ragged breathing subsided within a few seconds. He thought again of his duties and how long he had spent with her and that he really needed to get up and leave.

He heard her take a deep breath. She did not move to relinquish his place on the bed, or even the phallus growing languid within her. And then she spoke, her voice beautiful, sweet and childlike. A voice of love.

"You know why it was so important for me to make love to you again, Marty?"

". . . Why?"

She breathed again. "When you get over there to that place where everybody is dying, I want you to remember what it's like to be alive."

Chapter Six

"Are the red beans and rice made with animal fat?"

"Animal fat?"

"Well, pork is what I'm asking about. Are they cooked in oil made from animals?"

"Oh, no. All the oil we use in the kitchen is vegetable based."

"Okay then." Sam Tushmann closed his menu. "I'll have the red beans and rice and the garden salad with ranch."

"Have your salads right out, gentlemen," the server said. He scribbled down the last of their order, slid the menus under his arm and walked toward the kitchen.

"You take that pretty seriously?" Larsen asked. "The dietary restrictions?"

"Oh. Eating pork, you mean? Well, I suspect I would not be excluded from paradise for enjoying the occasional ham sandwich. However I never know when a member of the synagogue is sitting at the next table, listening to make sure I do everything Kosher."

"Kosher? This place isn't Kosher, is it? I live on their pork ribs and BLTs."

"No, I don't literally mean Kosher. I mean, I have to be circumspect. To maintain an air of proper respectability. At least wherever I might bump into some of the elect."

Larsen smiled broadly. "And here I thought that holding clergy to a higher standard than the Almighty expects of anybody else was just practiced by Christians."

He shook his head. "Nope. As one of my colleagues used to warn me, there are plenty of synagogues out there persecuting their rabbis for not being Christian enough."

They laughed together. Larsen leaned back in his chair, suddenly aware he wanted to confide in this friend. Wondering if he should.

"So . . . Sam, is this conversation privileged? Just between us?"

Tushmann's eyes narrowed slightly. He studied Larsen for a moment.

"Who is she?"

Larsen jumped. "Where'd you come up with that?"

The rabbi shrugged. "Well, I'm guessing your congregation doesn't have enough money to make it worth stealing. I've known you long enough to know you aren't any kind of an extremist or into kinky stuff. That pretty much only leaves 'the other woman.'"

". . . And this is confidential, right?"

Tushmann leaned forward conspiratorially. "I know it's none of my business, Martin, but are you circumcised?"

"I am, as a matter of fact."

"Well then I'm just going to pretend for the sake of discussion that I saw you in the men's room and mistook you for one of my flock. I am therefore bound. Everything we say stays right here over these bread sticks."

"All right. . . . I'm having an affair, Sam."

He nodded. "I see. And is this a woman in your church?"

Larsen shook his head. "Her mother was. Remember the funeral I did a couple weeks ago, Joan Celeste? That was her mother. Nobody in the church even knew that Ange existed. She just showed up after Joan lapsed into a coma. She got here with just enough time to set up the funeral before her mother died."

He gazed at his friend's face, watching for judgment or outrage, before he continued. "She asked me to come to her mother's place to pick up a few things she wanted to donate to the church."

". . . And one thing led to another?"

"And she had a magnum of my favorite wine waiting for me. And she was wearing the sexiest little black dress you ever saw—bra-less and extremely seductive."

"I take it you find her very attractive?"

"I find her exquisite. In every way. She's a counselor, Sam. She knows exactly what to say and when to say it. And she has some real ability in other ways as well."

Concern flashed across Tushmann's face. "So are you thinking of leaving your wife for this beautiful woman you've known for every bit of two weeks?"

He shook his head. "No. That's not in the cards. She's only going to be here for a few more days. Long enough to get her mom's estate disposed of. Then she's heading back to Florida." He sighed. "I guess this is actually more of a fling than an affair."

Sam pursed his lips. "Doesn't sound like you have much experience with this sort of thing."

"No. Nothing like this has ever happened to me before. Which is not to say that I haven't had women—and a few guys— come on to me in the churches I've served."

"It's an occupational hazard for clergy of all flavors, I suspect." The rabbi cocked his head. "So I'm flattered that you trusted me with this. I suppose this relationship you are having is not common knowledge. May I asked why you decided to tell me about this? Are you feeling some remorse about this—even though you know it's only a temporary relationship?"

"Maybe that's it—but in a backward sort of way." Larsen frowned. "It's not that I feel guilty about this. It's that I don't feel guilty. I feel worse about not feeling guilty than I do about making love to her. I probably should be riddled with fear and self-loathing. Instead I feel more . . . I don't know what to call it?"

"Excitement? Fulfillment?"

"Um, excited and satisfied. Yeah that. But I think more than anything what I feel is power."

"Power?"

"Yeah."

Sam studied his face. "So you're saying that this—what did you call her? Ang?"

"Ange. It's French."

"Okay. You're saying this woman empowers you. . . . And you don't feel all that guilty about your relationship with her?"

"Is that messed up or what?"

They laughed.

"Well," Sam spoke slowly, "this sort of makes you wonder if the real reason they caution clergy against extra-marital relationships is not because they are sinful, wicked and destructive, but because they expose clergy to awesome realities and emotions they otherwise would never experience."

Larsen chuckled. "You may be right about that, Sam. Of course, I still know beyond doubt that having an affair is destructive."

"Yes, it always does have that potential. . . . Just out of curiosity, why were you so willing to share this with me?"

He thought about the question. "For starters, there's really nobody else I can talk to about this. Mary-Martha would probably find it somewhat difficult to be objective regarding Ange. There's no way in hell I'd talk to any of my colleagues—dear souls that they are."

"You don't trust them?"

He shrugged. "Let's just say that, in the years to come, knowing this about me might tempt some among my colleagues to seek some sort of favor. Or they might ask me to enter into a conspiracy of some sort with them."

"You don't think I'm going to do that?"

"No, actually I don't. What sort of conspiracy could we ever have?"

"Yeah, I see what you mean. Still I'm sure I should be able to get some gain from this confession. I'll have to think it over and let you know."

"Um-hmm. Oddly enough, the person I think is most capable of being clear and objective about this is Ange. But how do you say to your lover , 'Help me figure out why having hot, erotic sex with you is so empowering when it should be so destructive?'"

"Yes. And what do you think she'd say if you asked her that?"

"She would say, 'It's just like you, Marty, to find a way to distract yourself from what's beautiful and enriching during these few, sweet moments we have together. I'll be gone for the rest of your life and you will have decades to figure us out, and whether or not you need to repent.'"

Sam nodded slowly. "Does this Ange have a sister?"

"Here is you dinner salad, sir, with ranch."

They jumped, startled as the waiter set the bowls before them.

"And here is you wedge salad with blue cheese, sir."

"Thanks."

"You meals will be out right away."

"Okay. Thanks."

Sam smiled at him. "BLT, huh? You say you love those, but you didn't order one. And you didn't get the bacon crumbles on your salad. Sounds like you didn't want to offend me."

"Well, it was just courtesy."

"I'm okay with you eating pork in front of me, Martin. But thanks for the thought."

69

"Are you okay with me having this steamy tryst with the world's most seductive woman and telling you about it?"

He dashed pepper on his salad. "As I say, I'm flattered that you trusted me with it. And I'm intrigued by it. I've had people tell me about a number of 'outside' relationships, but nothing like this. And you can come talk to me about it after it's all over. Like—" He glanced up at Larsen. "—after she's gone and suddenly you realize that you enjoy 'strange,' as they say, and you want more of that forbidden fruit. Most of all, I'm glad of one thing."

". . . Which is?"

"That you didn't ask me if I was ever with anyone outside my marriage."

The footsteps coming down the hall toward his study were not those of Horace, so he was not surprised when there was a knock before the door was opened. Larry Looper looked around the corner at him.

"Hi, Pastor. Do you have a moment?"

"Come in, Larry."

Looper slid into the armchair facing him. "So, I guess we need to talk about the fall fellowship assembly."

Larsen pursued his lips. "Do you mean, specifically, we need to discuss the menu the women are preparing for the meal?"

"Uh."

"Do you mean you think we should have rib eyes, baked potatoes, homemade dessert and everything else the bishop wants?"

"Uh. Yeah. That's what I wanted to talk about."

"First let me ask you this, Larry. Do you think a secretary who goes behind her boss' back to sabotage his decisions and instructions so she can curry favor with the bishop should be fired? And if not, then why not?"

Looper shrugged. "That's just Edith, just how she does. She's been here forever and we all understand that's how she acts."

"That's a description of her misbehavior, not a reason we should tolerate it."

The moderator waved his hand as if wiping away the topic. "That's not what I came here to discuss."

"I know that. But we should discuss it. If weren't for her insubordination, we wouldn't have anything to discuss."

"Look, Pastor, if we're going to host the assembly, we should go all out to support it."

"And having casseroles and staying within our budget is not supporting the synod?"

"We're not talking about any great extra expense here if we give the bishop what he wants."

"How great an expense are we talking about?"

"I don't know. A couple hundred dollars."

"And shall we take it out of the men's fellowship account?"

Looper stared, mouth open. "Why would we do that?"

"We have to get it somewhere. I have some version of this conversation every year at budget time, Larry. There is always some unexpected expense outside the budget. Somebody has overspent. We are always over budget. No department chair wants to take the hit, so the overage comes out of the general fund. Then when we start planning next year's expenses, someone on the stewardship department says, 'Oh, we're over budget. We can't afford to give the staff a raise. We can't afford to spend any more money on missions. Charity must begin at home, you know.'"

Hardness flashed across the moderator's face and his jaw tightened. "As long as we're putting our cards on the table, Pastor, I think it's only fair you should know that some of our members are complaining about you."

"Really? Is this more than the usual number of members who are complaining, given that somebody is always complaining about me?"

He arched his eyebrows. "I don't think you should be so cavalier about this, Pastor. These are the people who depend on you, look up to you and pay your salary."

"All right, Larry, what is the nature of their complaints?" The image of Ange—naked, her limbs wrapped around him—flashed through his mind.

"When we called you almost six years ago, Pastor, it was with the express intent of building up our congregation. Now, all this time later, we're at the same plateau we were on when you first arrived."

"Really?" He feigned surprise. "The number of total participating members when I first got here was 275. Now it's 317. Sounds like growth to me."

Doubt creased Looper's face. "I know it was more than 275 before you came."

"Not if you purged your rolls of the people who had moved away or hadn't been in church in ten years."

"Well, I know for sure it isn't 300—or more—today."

"Yes it is. You're only looking at 'giving units,' families that make a pledge. Six years ago we had seventy-seven giving units. Several of the more generous units died off and those who took their places don't give as much. But still, today there are eighty-four giving units."

Looper seemed confounded by the numbers, disbelieving them. "So, for the sake of argument, let's say you're correct—that we've increased—"

"Sixteen percent. We've had a net membership increase of sixteen percent."

"Well if your figures are correct—and they stand to be verified—that's still sort of paltry, don't you think? Somebody told me a growing church adds 10% a year."

"Really? You think our growth is paltry? Out of the 250 congregations in our synod, how many do you think have grown 16% in the last five reporting periods?"

"Uh—"

"Five. Well, seven if you count the two brand new church starts. And of those five, only St. Timothy's is more than fifty-years-old." He could feel his emotion rising, the tone of his voice growing more assertive. "That puts St. Timothy's in the top 3% of the synod when it comes to evangelical growth. And among churches older than you, we're number one."

The moderator responded with his own anger. "Now see here, Pastor, you can play with numbers all you want and make them appear in your favor, but the members of St. Timothy's expected real growth when you came and we just haven't seen it."

An odd feeling descended upon Larsen, one of strength and—simultaneously—candor. "Larry, I know you really well, but I'm still going to be honest with you. If you hooked the members of St. Timothy's up to a lie detector and asked them, 'Do you want our church to grow,' they would all say 'yes,' and the polygraph machine would say they were telling the truth. The reality is, however, that ever significant program I've tried to institute to build this church has been opposed and defeated."

". . . For instance?"

"For instance the summer day camp program: a safe place for parents to leave their kids during the summer and a dozen jobs for teenagers."

"Come on, Pastor, our insurance liability would have been through the roof."

"No it wouldn't," Larsen shook his head incredulously. "I disproved that before the vote was ever taken. The day camp rider on our insurance would have been paid for by net proceeds from the first week of camp. The council voted it down because they had no idea what sort of kids and parents it might bring to the church. The insurance thing was a straw man so nobody had to come out and say they were afraid to open the children's wing to anyone who might show up. And how about the mothers' neighborhood Bible study?"

"That wasn't really our program. Other churches had started that in downtown St. Louis and it just crept out to the county. Some of us had some real theological concerns about the curriculum."

"Horseshit, Larry. Some of our leaders didn't want poor, single mothers coming into the church on weeknights and bringing their kids into our nursery. Why, for all we knew, some of those folks might have been black."

"Have you lost it, Pastor? We have black and Asian members already."

"Yeah, and we're hoping to have a token Eastern European family—maybe even an Hispanic—one day, aren't we? But the one program we should really be talking about is the neighborhood advocacy program, Larry. You know, where we engage the congregation in learning about the needs of our entire community, then work with other churches to meet those needs and change the city for the better. Remember that—how you were in favor of it last year before you became moderator, then you shot it down this year?"

"Fir—First of all," Looper stammered, "when I fully understood the program, I saw where there were problems with it. Second, that program had nothing to do with evangelism. And thir—third, I was only one of the people on the council who voted against it."

He stared at the moderator for a moment, then held up one finger. "First, you understood that program perfectly last year and you were willing to support it before you actually had to take a stand on it and back me up in front of the congregation. Second, you and I both know the whole community would have seen St. Timothy in a new light—a very positive light that would have attracted people who want to see a little meat on the bones of their faith. And—" He held up a third finger. "—If the moderator speaks against something and votes against it, it tends to make other members of the council think there's something wrong with it. So you really had more than 'one vote' my friend." When Looper did not respond, he continued. "So about the congregation's criticism of me. Are people unhappy with my preaching?"

". . . Well, no."

"Do I fail them when it comes to pastoral care or fulfilling my priestly duties, like weddings and baptisms?"

"No, Pastor. No one has any complaints about that."

He drew a breath. "You know what I think, Larry? I think that, if I quit trying to instigate new programs that might build the church or even, perish the thought, build the Kingdom of God, I could stay here as long as I wanted to. 'Cause when you get down to brass tacks, the members of St. Timothy's like it just the way it is. And they don't want a lot of new strangers in the church, they just want enough squeaky clean Christians just like themselves so the church doesn't die."

The momentary silence allowed them to hear the weighty approaching footsteps of Horace Mixon. Larsen stared at the door, and Looper followed his gaze. There was the notorious pause between the last footfall and the door edging open, Horace's large face partially concealed.

"Uh, am I interrupting, Pastor?"

"Hello, Horace. I trust you have come to tell me that at last you have caught the rat."

The custodian sighed in disgust, straightened and stepped into the office. "No, Pastor. I came to tell you the rat is still eluding me. He has actually escalated his game."

Larsen's eyebrows arched. "Do tell? How does a rat become more of a rat?"

"Brazen. He's got more brazen, Pastor. He drags different food containers out of the pantry, chews holes in them and leaves them all around the church. And he attacks any time of day—broad daylight. Edith left her lunch bag sitting on the kitchen counter yesterday morning. When she came back to get it at lunch time, the rat had chewed a hole through the sack and ate part of her chicken sandwich."

"Hmm. Chicken? This may be a Methodist rat we're dealing with here. Are you still just baiting the three traps?"

"No, I've got five traps out. I also set out two of those adhesive traps—you know, the ones with the stick 'em? He got into one of them in the pantry and I found it upside down in the choir room. With rat hair in it. Somehow he prized it off."

"I know you take this as your personal responsibility, Homer, but is it time for us to call in the professionals?"

He shook his head rapidly. "No, sir, Pastor. He's escaped me thus far, but I'll get him in the end."

Larsen's rectum tingled. "So are you resorting to poison, then?"

"No, never poison. He'd go off inside a wall and die somewhere and we'd smell him for months. He'd get the last laugh. No, I'm staying after him. Eventually he's going to take one of my traps for granted and then I'll get him."

"I hope you do, Horace," Looper said. "Mrs. Eidebeck got a flea bite in the fellowship hall last Sunday. That flea had to come from the rat."

"That is distressing," Larsen said, "when the rat's poor hygiene begins to impact the saints of the church."

His intercom buzzed. The three men looked at it simultaneously. Larsen leaned over and pressed the response button.

"Yes, Edith, what can I do for you?"

"Sorry, Pastor, but hospice just called, the way you asked them to notify you, you know? Jewel Vonnegut just passed away. Her family is gathering. They'd like you to come say a prayer before they take the body."

"Are they still on the phone?"

"Yes, Pastor."

"Please tell them I'm leaving now and am on my way."

"Yes, sir."

He gazed at the two men who stood staring at him. "If you will excuse me, fellows. The cloth calls. Uh, Horace?"

"Yes, Pastor."

"I would really prefer it if, when you come to my office door, you'd knock before you come in."

The custodian's eyes widened. "Don't I do that already? Why sure, Pastor, I'll be glad to knock first."

"Thanks to Misty, our soloist, and to Kosmo for accompanying her on the organ. I know that 'A Mighty Fortress' was cherished by Jewel, as by all of us in the church family. Also, Tim, I speak for everyone when I say you did a marvelous job. What a difficult thing it is to eulogize someone you love and are close to, someone you've known all your life. Even more so when it's your grandmother. I know that, in the heavenly places, Jewel is rejoicing and smiling at your warm remembrance. I had not heard the story of how she got the apple cake recipe, though, like everyone else at St. Timothy's, I really enjoyed the very generous portions she brought to our annual Palm Sunday luncheon.

"This week, as I meditated on the life of Jewel Vonnegut—rich in years and replete in the ups and downs of human living—I found myself drawn to a passage of scripture, a text that I know from our many visits was a personal favorite of hers. This brief passage seems so reflective of her experiences, simple and elegant—just like Jewel herself.

"Often times we churchgoers hear a scripture again and again, and it becomes familiar to us. Indeed we hear it so many times that we get a little complacent about its divine meaning, its importance to us and our faith. We think we understand everything there is to know about it, that it has nothing fresh or relevant to say to us. Oddly enough, it's when we reach the point of 'familiarity breeds contempt,' that we need to stop and listen closely. There may be greater, vastly important truths we are overlooking in that familiar scripture. It might still have lessons to teach us.

"There is no better example of this than Jewel's favorite psalm, the foundation of our message today: Psalm 23. I believe the great King David sang this psalm toward the end of his long, rather complicated life. He was trying to express the relationship he had with God. And as he considered the multitude of triumphs and tragedies and poignant moments of his days, David was inevitably drawn back to his youth as a shepherd boy. 'That's it!' he exclaimed. 'All my life, God has been my shepherd.'

"Thus he writes, 'The Lord is my shepherd. I shall not want. He makes me lie down in green pastures. He leads me beside still waters. He restores my souls. He leads me in the path of righteousness for his namesake.' In these magnificent, simple words, David created an indelible image. As he hear his words, how clearly we can see a mountaintop meadow where a flock of lambs frolics, grazing on the sweetest green clover and drinking cool water from a pool that is absolutely clear and still. How the lambs run and play, until at length they lie down in the gentle sun and sleep. And watching over this idyllic scene, silent and peaceful, is the shepherd, leaning upon his staff as he observes these little ones for whom he has provided so abundantly.

"I think we all have times—blissful, joyous times—just as David describes here. Jewel certainly did. Did you ever know anyone who rejoiced in living each day more than she did? Jewel found superb joy in so many of the common things we tend to take for granted. I never knew anyone who was happy scrubbing the sinks in the church kitchen, but she relished it. 'I tell people there is a right and wrong way to do this,' she told me a couple years ago, 'but honestly I just enjoy cleaning the kitchen.' And if the mundane tasks of life brought her pleasure, you can imagine how she felt about getting together with her family. Jewel came breezing into the pastor's study last Thanksgiving as giddy with excitement as any school girl. 'I promised to prepare the Eucharist this Sunday, Pastor,' she said, 'but I can't. My daughter Ellen is taking me to Rockport this weekend to see her grandkids.' I only knew Jewel for a half dozen years, but those who knew her for a lifetime have testified to me that she was always that way. From her childhood, she was a happy person who appreciated whatever goodness each day brought her. Jewel enjoyed the beauty of life and she knew where it came from. In this, her life is a lesson to us, a confirmation that God blesses each of us with a multitude of mountaintop days, full of light and love, and we are to grasp and relish those blessings.

"King David, as he continued to sing the psalm, painted for us a second image of our Creator. 'Yea, though I walk through a valley as dark as death, I shall fear no evil, for you are with me. Your rod and staff, they comfort me.' As we hear these words, we realize this is about the same flock, the same shepherd, but the scene has changed dramatically. An afternoon thunderstorm has risen unexpectedly, something that might happen suddenly on the mountain. As the heavy clouds roll in, they block out the sun, so that the midday has become as dark as night. With the storm looming, the shepherd knows he must lead his lambs down the mountain to the safety of the sheepfold below. Lightning flashes about the lambs as they descend through the narrow pathways. Rain pelts them. Danger surrounds them. In the darkness, how easy it would be for a lamb to wander too close to the edge of the precipice and fall to its death. And lurking unseen in the shadows are the predators of that wilderness, wolves, wild dogs and even lions, waiting for a lamb to draw near enough to be snatched by the throat and dragged away. Still, in the face of all that might terrify them, the flock remains calm. In the depths of their being, they realize the shepherd knows the safe pathway down the mountain. They know that if, in a momentary lapse one might come precariously close to the cliff, with his shepherd's staff, he will draw the little one safely back to him. They know that, should a destroyer leap out at them, with his mighty staff the shepherd will strike and kill it. Despite all the turmoil and the potential for harm, the flock is secure within the protection of the shepherd.

"I suspect all of us, like King David, know what it is to experience the presence and protection of the Lord in our moments of greatest travail. Jewel Vonnegut certainly did, even as young woman. Her parents, I'm told, did not want Jewel to marry Herm way back in 1942. Here was this Marine about to head off to parts unknown to fight in a World War. They did their best to convince her to wait until the war was over. Jewel told her mom and dad that she wanted to give Herm a wife to come home to, a 'reason to return,' as she said it. For three long years—going for months at a time without hearing from her groom or knowing where he was or what he was facing—Jewel staunchly held onto her trust that he was coming back to her. And of course he did. The marriage that her parents resisted so stoutly managed to last for sixty years and to produce this beautiful loving family. As she told me that story, I said, 'So you kept your faith through that difficult time.' 'No,

Pastor,' she retorted. 'Faith kept me.' What a lovely way Jewel had of expressing just what King David has said. In our most difficult, dangerous passages, we must remember we have a shepherd who is capable of leading us safely down the mountain.

"That's not the end of the psalm, though, is it? David has shared one final vision of the Shepherd God with us: 'You prepare a table for me in the presence of my enemies. You anoint my head with oil. My cup overflows. Surely goodness and mercy shall follow me all the days of my life and I shall dwell in the house of the Lord for ever.' A very different scene is pictured in these words. You know, an 'eye for eye' was the custom in that day. Can you imagine how easy it might have been for someone to bring injury or even cause the death of another person unintentionally. And if you did hurt or kill someone in this way, the family of the victim had the right to pursue you and take equal recompense upon you. In these last verses of Psalm 23, we are hearing the story of a fugitive. Someone is fleeing across the wilderness. Perhaps this is a person who has accidentally caused the death of someone and the family of the victim is pursuing this man—slowly, inexorably drawing closer and closer to him. As he strength and endurance ebb, there in the distance he sees the tent of a shepherd. He knows the law. If he can get to that tent, those chasing him can do him no harm so long as the shepherd is willing to offer him hospitality. With this hope in his heart, the fugitive runs toward the distant shepherd's tent and grasps it just as he reaches the point of exhaustion. For a moment he is safe, but he wonders, 'Will the shepherd offer me hospitality?' Slowly, making sure not to lose contact with the walls of the tent, he makes his way around to the open front and anxiously gazes inside.

"There in the coolness of the tent to his astonishment he sees a great table, spread with a sumptuous feast. And seated behind the table is the shepherd—the very same shepherd we know from the glorious mountaintop and the dark valley. And the shepherd rises and extends his arms. 'My son,' he says, 'I have been waiting for you. Sit here at my table and be refreshed.' Amazed at this abundant welcome, this fugitive sits at the table and partakes of the wonderful food and drink throughout the day. He eats until he is sated and renewed. But then, in the gathering darkness, he looks out and sees, sitting and waiting, those who want to claim his life.

It is then the shepherd rises and pours oil on the man's head—a sign of adoption. He fills the man's cup to overflowing with wine—a sign of hospitality. 'My son,' the shepherd says, 'you have nothing to fear. You may dwell here with me forever.'

". . . You know, we're all fugitives, aren't we? The same enemy is pursuing all of, slowly, inexorably closing in on us. And those of us who have lived long enough to witness all the inevitabilities of life know that ultimately there is one enemy we cannot elude. Jewel knew that. Eighteen months ago when she was first diagnosed with leukemia, she understood that this day was coming. Those of us who knew her were not surprised that she never stopped being the joyous woman of faith who loved every single day of life. Yes, we knew that she knew her shepherd and she was headed toward that welcoming table, that grand feast, the shepherd had promised her. Jewel had a deep awareness her shepherd was saving a place for her at the table. She was eager to sit at that table with Herm and with her brother and sisters and her parents and so many friends. Jewel Vonnegut knew our shepherd very well. Today, by her example, she speaks to us and says, 'Do not overly grieve. We'll meet and embrace once again. And I'm saving you a seat at the table.' Amen."

Chapter Seven

It occurred to him, as she pressed him gently against the back of the apartment door, kissing him while she unbuttoned his shirt, that every time with Ange was different.

When she opened the door on Monday afternoon, the interior of the apartment was completely dark. She pulled him inside, closed the door and pushed him against it and began to kiss him. As quickly as it happened, he was still able to see she was wearing a floor length white nightgown with bare shoulders. The light, smooth fabric casually followed the contours of her body without revealing its particulars, apart from the two maddening protrusions of her breasts, each crowned with a nickel-sized disk.

She seemed not in a hurry as she undressed him, pausing from her kiss to pull off his shirt. Ange pressed her lips to his, her tongue into his mouth as she unzipped his pants and slid them and his underwear down to his ankles. Without speaking, she knelt and pulled off his shoes and socks and freed his limbs of this clothing, so that he stood naked before her. She took a half step back, as if evaluating him, then pulled her gown over her head and let it fall to the floor.

Turning wordlessly, she took his hand and led him into the bedroom. It was strangely innocent to him, as if one child found the other for whom she had been sent and was bringing him to their appointed place. The bedspread had been pulled back on one corner, in invitation. She dropped his hand and climbed up on the bed and turned to look at him. Larsen slid the bedspread back and sat on the bed beside her.

Ange maneuvered him to the center of the bed and made him lie flat on his back. She kissed his neck and throat. Straddling him, she spread his hands and began to kiss his face, his forehead, his cheeks, all the while the lips of her vagina caressed his penis, sliding along it, seeming to take it in and then lifting away from it. He felt his member straighten and lengthen. Raising her head, she sighed, one breast dangling before him, the nipple a dark stalk. He reached up for it with his lips, but she pushed his head flat against the pillow.

Sliding languorously down his legs toward the foot of the bed, she kept her eyes—smoldering with intent—locked on his. The strength of her grip when she grasped his cock surprised him and made him jump, and Ange smiled. She ran her hands the length of the engorged shaft once and again, slowing as she watched the clear rivulet of pre cum emerge and drip slowly down his glans. Lowering her head, she took him into her mouth, sucking fiercely, pressing her tongue against him, moving up and down with excruciating sloth. And as he watched, she reached down to her own sex and manipulated her clitoris, spreading her legs in response to her touch. He watched her in silent, throbbing, glorious arousal.

Ange raised her head away from his member abruptly. She smacked her lips. Crawling forward, she kissed him, pressing herself against him—breasts against his chest, effluent crevice against his rock hard, dripping wet cock. Then at last she spoke to him, whispering in his ear.

"Now you can fuck me, baby."

Larsen put his hands on her hips and positioned her so their genitals embraced. Ange reached down and guided him, sighing and closing her eyes as he entered her. Her behind rose and fell in concert with his upward pulses. For minutes they continued in the one position, her astride him, his hands on her breasts, nipples between his fingers, the tiny beads of arousal pale against the darkened aureoles.

At length she closed her eyes again and raised her head. "Forgive me, love, but I feel like I'm a little squirty today. At least I'm incredibly wet. . . . And one other thing."

". . . Which is?"

"I'm about to cream all over you."

"Cream on, my love. . . . 'Cause I'm about thirty seconds from creaming in."

She twitched suddenly, arching her back and pressing down, her inner lips taut against his anxious penis. As she had said, he could feel a warm wave flow from within her, spilling down the shaft of his member and into his pubic hair.

"Oh. Oh. Oh." He moaned and pounded himself up and into her as the orgasm descended upon him. It burst from him as he thrust upward again and again, holding her hips tightly against him. "Mmm. Mmm."

Ange collapsed atop him, quivering, drawing ragged animal breaths. Larsen, head back and limbs askew, closed his eyes. For minutes they lay in a serene heap, the silence broken only by the diminishing of their labored breathing. The only discernible movement was the maddening slide of fluid down the inside of his thigh.

At length she drew a long, relaxed breath and, without raising her head, asked, "So. How was your funeral?"

He chuckled, the motion causing her to jiggle against him. "Well technically, love, it wasn't my funeral." He thought about the question. "It was okay, I guess. . . . Jewell was a sweet, uncomplicated person and we sent her off with a lovely farewell."

"Sent her to heaven, did you?"

"Ha. Skeptical, are you?"

He could feel her shake her head. "I'm not disagreeing with you, Marty. I'm just wondering what you really believe. Do you think Jewell went to heaven when she died? . . . I mean, I know that's the official party line and all, but is that what you believe?"

He frowned. "Fortunately it doesn't matter what I believe."

She raised her head and looked into his eyes. "So! I'm not the skeptic. You are."

Larsen chuckled again. "Well, I believe her consciousness survived and went somewhere."

". . . Like, Palm Springs?"

He laughed, reaching out for her arm and holding her on top of him. "If we get a choice, I'd much rather go to Santa Fe. Or maybe San Francisco."

"You don't believe in heaven? You don't think there's a glorious place in the clouds where God brings everybody who makes him happy?"

Drawing a slow breath, he said, "Well that's two questions, isn't it, Ange? I do believe in an afterlife, yes. Do I believe in heaven?" He shook his head. "That part I'm real unclear about. I don't think anybody knows what heaven is like. I don't believe we spend an eternity just praising God."

"Really. And why not?"

"Well." He shrugged. "That would be closer to hell, wouldn't it? I mean, if you consider all the glories, mysteries and wonders of creation—just in the part that we know about—and yet instead of going off across the galaxies and dimensions exploring and learning and enjoying, we're supposed to sit around on clouds and glorify God. Despite what the song says, after 10,000 years of praising, that would get old for me. . . . Then too, there is some indication that there may be more than one layer to the afterlife."

"You mean like purgatory?"

"Oh hell no," he said sharply. "That's strictly an authoritarian invention to keep the sheep in line. I mean, there are very ancient and very recent accounts of multiple degrees or levels in the afterlife."

"Like the Mormons' belief that there are separate heavens for different groups—and they get top billing for themselves?"

"What preachershit. No. Have you heard of about 'near death experiences'?"

"Of course. I'm a counselor."

"So people talk about seeing this place of incredible beauty where everyone is young and lovely and healthy."

"Yeah?"

"But there are also cases where people talk about going beyond that, going beyond creation itself to a place that's a void. And the Creator dwells there in the void. . . . People who have gone there say they have asked God—although they say even the word 'God' doesn't capture the awesomeness of the Creator—and they ask whatever questions they want. . . . And God answers. Then they come back here."

". . . And they have all the answers?"

"Ha. No. Apparently the human mind cannot comprehend or retain the answers God gives them." He gazed into her eyes. "Like, the bodies and minds we possess limit the degree to which we can grasp ultimate realities." He looked back up at the ceiling. "Still, people who go there and come back are changed. They seem to have a new, permanent outlook on life."

"I see," she said slowly. "How does this all square with your theology?"

"Well, my dear, I'm afraid there is always a disconnect between theology and reality."

"Do tell? You mean—all these religions and all these denominations and all these prophets and preachers and professors—none of them got it right?"

"Nope. Not a one."

"I see. And how is that you were blessed with this divine knowledge?"

Larsen shook his head. "I suspect I'm not the only one who's figured this out. This was no special dispensation. No blinding revelation. I just gradually got to a point where I quite denying the obvious."

"The obvious?"

"Think about it, Ange. Can you think of any religion that doesn't have absurd beliefs? And mine is no different. I was preparing for a sermon a few years ago and suddenly it dawned on me that people who lived in ancient Greece, in ancient Rome, had the same degree of devotion to the pantheon that we Christians have to the Trinity in the 21st century. To us, belief in Zeus or Jupiter and all those gods is absurd. Only, we have no more objective justification for our belief in Christ than they did for believing in the Olympians."

"I thought religion was supposed to be a matter of faith in the unseen."

"What a dodge." He raised his head and looked at her. "Okay, so in your practice when a patient does something totally irrational just for the benefit of a lover or a spouse—like when they go back to an abusive husband or they give money to a spouse, knowing they're going to squander it on drugs or something—and you ask them to explain why they did it, what do they say?"

She shrugged. "Always. They say, 'Because I love him.'"

"Exactly! When you have no defense for the purely emotionally driven decision you make for the person you sleep with, you say, 'Because I love him.' Saying, 'because I love him' is just another way of saying, 'I have no defensible reason for what I did.' Well the same is true in religion. Try to pin down a conservative Christian about how they know the Bible is inerrant truth or that their peculiar set of behaviors or beliefs—like not letting women speak in church or condemning homosexuality—and they will invariably say that it's a matter of faith. 'Faith' is the answer that means they don't have an answer. People believe what they believe because somebody handed it down to them as the truth. And those who had it before them had no real justification for believing it either. I always love it when church leaders appeal to tradition. It's like saying, 'We've believed this fucked up bullshit for forty generations, so you should believe it too. That way we don't have to deal with the very real possibility that what we try real hard to believe is nonsense.'" He shook his head and lay back down.

"So," she said at length, "you don't believe in theology and spirituality at all?"

"Oh yes I do." He nodded. "I believe deeply that there are spiritual realities and there is theological truth." There was a wistful, longing note to his voice as he continued. "I believe in miracles and serendipity and a loving God. I believe we can discover truth about the spiritual world. Truths about our Creator. . . . I think people have had revelations over the millennia and they have tried to hold onto those snippets of the truth. The problem is that, invariably, they get to a point of saying that what they have is the exclusive truth. The ultimate truth. The only truth and everybody else is just . . . sucking hind teat."

She laughed, raising her head. "Haven't heard that one in a while."

"Well. At a certain point every religion goes from being description—telling about the great revelation that came to their founder—and instead they start being prescriptive. They tell people they have a lock on God. A lock on heaven. A lock on revelation. A lock on prayer. On salvation."

". . . Well then. So your opinion is that no religion will ever fully be able to apprehend the truth and, actually, religions prevent people from being aware from God."

"Yes," he nodded. "Religion does keep people away from God. Church is one of the best places to hide out from a genuine encounter with the Holy. But—" His expression grew intense. "—it doesn't have to be that way. . . . You see, the whole 'it's all a matter of faith' thing is a way of inhibiting true spiritual investigation."

Her voice tinged with mockery, she said, "Spiritual investigation? You mean like séances and voodoo?"

"No. I mean like genuine scientific investigation. You know, back in the Dark Ages, medicine was caught up in superstition. People believed that illness came from humors or winds or demons. Eventually medicine gradually broke away from the domain of superstition and began to dwell in the domain of science. And the result is that human beings—for all our pollution, stress, tobacco and gunpowder—live twice as long as we did before medicine went scientific."

She stared at him. "So you think you can scientifically investigate God?"

"Yep. Spirituality. I think we can. I mean . . . we already know—it's been scientifically demonstrated—that praying for sick people improves their chances of getting well. Why not investigate the reasons for that? The same way medicine once was the slave of superstition, spirituality is the slave of superstition. I just wonder what we might discover if, you know, it weren't."

Ange rubbed her chin, considering him with a skeptical look. "How things have changed for us, Marty. The first time we spoke, you were all about high Christian theology and platitudes. Remember how you told me about how wearing 'the cloth' imparted a divine calling to you? . . . And now you're the one saying you think that's all bunk."

"Bunk? . . . I guess that's what I'm saying. In a way. But I also know that Jewell's family needed the assurances I had to give them at the service. The peace and hope they took away were real. And in the final analysis, I think whatever world Jewell stepped into when she left this one is actually a whole lot better than anything I promised. No harp, no crown, no wings, no streets of gold—but maybe something a whole, whole lot better. And I'm not sure anything I could have said would have brought her family any more comfort or promise." He smiled at her. "You see, our bullshit is closer to the truth than anybody else's."

She laughed. "Oh my Marty." She extended her hand, running it along his smooth face tenderly. "So what do your colleagues think of this divergent spirituality of yours?"

Larsen shook his head slowly. "Before you came into my life, Ange, I had no one I could share this with."

"No one?"

"Nope."

"Not Mary-Martha?"

"Heavens no. She would consider my beliefs an affront to her parents."

"Oh. That's right her dad was a pastor too. . . . What about your bishop? Isn't he theologically profound."

"Ha! Poor Richard. What a dunce. If he were alone with God in an elevator, he wouldn't recognize him."

Her eyebrows rose. "Do tell?"

Larsen sat gazing at Sam Tushman.

The rabbi stared, emotionless, at the closed menu on the table before him. He did not raise his eyes or give any indication of willingness to converse.

"If I were paranoid . . ." Larsen said quietly.

Tushman glanced up at him.

"I would think my recent confession, while good for my soul, has driven a wedge between us."

He chuckled, "No Martin. Not at all." Tushman's head drooped to one side. "By the way, how is that working out for you?"

Larsen nodded. "The girl is leaving. . . . Actually, I'm feeling some grief. It's like, like . . . summer is coming. And I don't want spring to be over."

The server appeared at their table. "Have you had a chance to look at the menu?"

"Red beans and rice for me. A side salad with—oh—thousand island. And just tea to drink," Tushman said.

"I'm having the BLT and fries . . . and a Coke float."

The rabbi laughed. "You rebel!"

"You only live once."

"I'll put this order in and the food will be right out."

Larsen waited until the young man was gone, then looked back to his friend. "So if my dalliance isn't the source of your brooding, then allow me to boldly go where no pastor has gone before and ask what's bothering you."

Tushman drew a long breath. "For the first time since I was a kid in Sabbath school, I have a nearly irresistible urge to do physical harm to someone."

"Ah. And have I met this congregant?"

He shook his head. "He's not a member of the synagogue. He's my associate rabbi."

"Danny?"

"Rabbi Silver." He nodded slowly. "You know that big plate glass window that overlooks the meditation garden?"

"Yes."

He sighed. "I keep resisting the urge to throw his patoot right through that."

"I see, Sam. And may I ask why?"

Tushman leaned forward, speaking with an intensity Larsen had never experienced from him. "The little bastard thinks he knows everything. He has this attitude that he alone knows what it means to be Jewish, about our heritage, about what our congregation is doing wrong. . . . He makes major changes in our programs without asking permission. He starts new projects without approval. Just nine months out of seminary and the Holy One has sent him to save Judaism."

"Hmm. I take it he doesn't follow your leadership very well."

"Apparently he got the idea that, despite my title, my doctorate and my two decades of professional experience, he and I are equals. He believes my instructions are suggestions. He believes the council is quaint and has no authority over an august servant of the Most High."

Larsen toyed with the pepper shaker. "So how long has he been with you?"

"Six weeks."

"So that's kind of strange, isn't it? I mean, didn't he get ordained last summer? So what was he doing for the first six or seven months of his rabbinate?"

"Getting fired from his first charge."

"Oh!" Larsen laughed. "I got it. And let me guess, getting fired wasn't his fault?"

"Of course not. That temple was mired in old thinking and run by unfaithful people."

"Right. . . . So this kid is eaten up with 'seminarian's disease.'"

"What?"

"Seminarian's disease."

"It's when a student comes out of divinity school and gets ordained and believes that he or she has all the answers. It's like all wisdom and worship began with them. They are consumed with self-importance, righteous indignation and pitiful scorn for anyone who doesn't see the faith the way they do. They are impervious to leadership."

Slowly Tushman's face eased into a smile.

"Until this moment, Sam," Larsen said, "I thought this was strictly a Christian illness. I'm sorry to say, however, that the disease has spread to the Hebrew clergy as well."

"Uh huh. And people with this disease, do they end up in the emergency room sliced up and stuck full of window glass?"

He shrugged. "On those occasions when they do, they never understand why."

Tushman sighed again. "I have given this considerable thought. As perverse as this little shit is, the instant I lay a hand on him—I mean, just publicly explode in anger, not even beat him to a pulp like he deserves—it becomes my fault and my problem. . . . I suppose I could poison him."

"No," Larsen shook his head. "The folks who are trying to get rid of our church rat say that Rabbi Danny would just go die in the woodwork somewhere and stink for months. Do you seriously want my advice? I don't want to interfere."

"I would love any insight into how to handle this kid."

"Well, here's what I would do," Larsen said. "Get your Moderator—Board Chair—"

"President of the synagogue."

"Yeah. Get that person and tell him exactly how frustrated you are and why. Then tell him precisely what you're going to tell the kid and that he is going to back you up. Then the two of you get Danny alone and, remembering to remain as calm as possible— you're holding all the trump cards, remember—you tell him exactly what behavior you expect from him. Let me guess he's in some probationary period."

"Six months."

"Remind him that he can be summarily dismissed in the next six months and any deviation from your expectations will result in his immediate dismissal."

"Well he's going to say—"

"Yeah, I know. It's not open for discussion. I would say, 'Rabbi Silver, the first rule of any profession is to act in a professional manner. If you can't follow my instructions as I give them to you, then you will not succeed here. And based on your track record so far, the rabbinate may not be for you at all.' Then you might suggest he might be better suited wandering the Holy

Land, looking for disciples. And for women to pay all his expenses."

Tushman broke into laughter. "Well, that's how Jesus got his start, I'm told."

"Yeah, well, apparently Dan thinks he's already Messianic."

The rabbi leaned back. "So, my friend. I think that's probably . . . spot on. I will do what you suggest. . . . And what about you?"

"Me?"

"Don't you have some shitty folks in your parish who need to be confronted just so?"

Larsen stared at him, then began to shake his head slowly. "No, I just give advice, brother. Perish the thought I would take it."

"Why don't you ever want to make love anymore?"

He pushed the mute on the TV remote, dropped his Sudoku book and turned to Mary-Martha. "What?"

"Do you realize how long it's been since we had sex?"

He stared at her. ". . . How long?"

"Like three weeks."

"Really?" He pursed his lips. "So, do you want to?"

"Yeah, kinda. Usually you're the one who asks, though. Why haven't you?"

He shrugged. "Guess I've had a lot on my mind."

She sat forward in the bed. Her breasts, voluminous and unrestrained, rolled beneath her pajama top. "Like what?"

". . . The church rat." He drew a breath. "Sort of ironic, huh? When there's a rat loose in the church, you'd think pussy would be the only thing I was thinking of."

Mary-Martha laughed. She leaned toward the overnight stand and turned off the lamp. As she pulled her top over her head, Larsen turned off the television and dropped the remote and the puzzle magazine on his nightstand. When he turned back toward her, her form was scarcely visible in the darkness.

Caution ran through him. There were those positions and stimulations Ange shared with him that had never occurred between him and Mary-Martha. He would have to be cautious not to do anything to which his wife was not accustomed. Also he would have to be careful not to speak. Were there things he said to

Ange, names he called her, that he dared not let slip to now? And for the first time he wondered about diseases. What if Ange carried some sexually transmitted infection that he had picked up without realizing it?

As he pulled off his pajamas, Mary-Martha moved toward him. She caressed his bare chest and kissed the side of his face. He dropped his clothing on the side of the bed and turned to her, sliding his hand along her chest and gripping one large, round breast. How differently the two women were constructed—Ange lean and lithe, Mary-Martha round and voluptuous. And she, who for so many years had been his sole, dedicated partner, in this dark encounter seemed strange to him.

He pulled at one nipple with his lips, sucking it against his tongue while she slid down in the bed and spread her legs. He felt her grope for his penis and grip it.

"Wow," she said. "That was quick. I guess you are ready."

"What about you?" he whispered. Tenderly he manipulated her clitoris, letting his finger slip within her outer labia, lingering there until he felt the growing wetness.

A deep sound of assent gurgled up from her chest. "I'm ready and you're ready, Martin."

He kissed her and held the kiss as he entered her. As she relaxed he slipped fully into her. For a moment he did not move, savoring their coming together. Then he began slowly to raise and lower his hips. Mary-Martha turned her head to the side, her arms around his shoulders. Sound came from her, a serene cooing sound. Yes, this was how she responded when they made love.

Larsen felt as if he were watching them making love from somewhere outside himself. He had an odd mastery of himself this night, almost as if he could have copulated for hours, as if he could lure this seldom-orgasmic woman into coming again and again. And so he was not surprise after ten minutes that she began to clutch at him, to pull him and push him away, to squirm against him.

"Ooo. Ooo."

. Then came an explosion of air from her vagina. It convulsed around his penis. Mary-Martha relaxed, quivered and relaxed completely, her limbs spread. And, taking short, hard strokes, Larsen came as well, holding himself within her for a minute or so before rolling over onto his side of the bed.

". . . That was good, Martin."

He nodded in the darkness. "Really good. Was it worth the wait?"

He felt her head loll toward him. "Well yes, but I bet it can be that good without waiting a month."

He laughed.

"I've got to go the bathroom," she said lazily. "But first I'm going to lay here for a minute."

Within a few seconds she was snoring. Larsen smiled, wondering at the satisfaction he felt, wondering if he should instead be riddled with guilt. Guilt for what exactly? Was he now cheating on Ange? She wouldn't expect him not to have sex with his wife, would she?

As he lay waiting for sleep, thinking about his wife and his lover, he remembered suddenly what Ange had asked him the afternoon before, just after they made love: "So. How was your funeral?" And it dawned on him, he had never told her he had conducted a funeral.

Chapter Eight

Annie Dulce set the cup of steaming tea before her pastor and eased herself laboriously into the armchair facing him.

"How's your back, Annie?"

"Miserable. Same old same old." She smiled at him. "Got my third shot last week. The one that was supposed to work, you know."

"But it isn't?" He slid a half teaspoon of sugar into the tea and stirred it.

"Oh hell no." Her hand wavered as she held her own cup and saucer and blew across the mouth of it. "It's sort of humorous, Pastor, in a pathetic way."

"Why do you say that?"

"Oh." She chuckled. "That young doctor. I have grandchildren older than that pup. He has me lying on my side on the table. And he says, 'Now this may hurt, Mrs. Dulce.' And I think, 'Oh yeah? Is it going to hurt worse than it already hurts?' . . . Wasn't that bad. Didn't work though."

"So what's next?"

She swung her head broadly from side to side. "Ain't nothing next, Pastor." When he didn't respond, she said, "The next thing would be to fuse the vertebra in my back. But they can't do that."

"Why not?"

"They're afraid my heart will stop during the operation."

"Oh."

"You remember I got a bad heart, right?"

"Yes ma'am. I was there for your oblation and pacemaker, remember?"

"Of course I do. I don't have Alzheimer's. Or if I do, I forgot."

He laughed. "I think you're sharp as a tack, ma'am. So what will they do about your back?"

"Painkillers." She sipped her tea. "Strong ones. I asked what would happen if I got addicted. For some reason they thought that was real funny."

Larsen refrained from smiling. "I see. There's no aggressive treatment they can pursue to prevent the pain?"

94

"No."

They sat in silence, looking into their teacups.

She asked, "How are your wife and girls?"

"They're doing real good."

"Are Donna and Daphne looking forward to school being out?"

"I don't know about that, but their mother sure is. She's not teaching summer school this year. She has informed me that we are taking a two consecutive week family vacation."

"Oh really," Annie said, "and what if I die while you're gone?"

He leaned toward her, narrowing his eyes. "You wouldn't dare."

She giggled.

"Well what about your family? Are your great-grandkids coming to see you when school's out?"

Annie looked past him. Somehow his words had stirred something—sadness perhaps—in her.

"Should I have not asked that, Annie? Did I touch a nerve there?"

Her lips pursed, she said, "You know where Barbara lives, right? In Olathe?"

"Yes. Over by Kansas City, isn't it?"

"Yes. Both her girls live around there. All on the Kansas side. . . . They want to move me out there."

Unsurprised, he raised his eyebrows. "Oh?"

"Oh yes. They have a nursing home all picked out for me."

"Nursing home, Annie? Do you mean a retirement community?"

"Hmm. Retirement home. Assisted living. Reform school—"

He laughed.

"Call it whatever you want, Pastor. It's locking the old lady up."

"I don't think that's their intent, Annie."

She blew across the top of her cup. "At least I don't have to worry about learning my way around a great big city. They're going to take away my car."

"Really? I thought your doctor had been asking you to quit driving months ago."

95

"You know where I drive, Pastor? To the grocery store, the beauty parlor and the church. And my car knows the way to all those places."

"That's all?" His voice was skeptical. "Somebody told me they saw you driving to that big casino up on the Missouri."

She giggled girlishly. "You know that's not true, Pastor."

"That's what I told 'em. . . . So, Barbara wants you to move out west."

Annie nodded slowly. "And give up . . . my house, my car, my church . . . all my friends." She began to weep.

Larsen sighed. "I'm so sorry Annie."

She sniffed. Producing a hanky from somewhere, she dabbed her eyes and wiped her nose. "Well, doesn't look like the old lady has a choice, now does it, Pastor?"

"Have you and Barbara thought about a retirement village here. Manchester has a couple nice places."

"Doctor says—" She lowered her face, crying again for a long minute. "I should be in a home where they have different levels of care. He says I should be able to go from assisted living all the way to skilled care without having to move all around. And Barbara says—" She choked back her words.

"I suppose it would be very difficult for Barbara and your granddaughters if they had to make a lot trips to St. Louis." He nodded. "I guess I understand that. Is there a plan for when all this is going to happen, Annie?"

Her body shuddered with the deep breath she drew. "I'm on a list at this place right there in Olathe. They're guessing about six to eight weeks. The name of the home is Golden Prairie Homestead. . . . Pastor, did you ever hear of such a goddamn stupid name for a nursing home in all your life?"

He laughed aloud. "I guess they're trying to make it sound appealing."

"Well, I told Barbara they better do a better job of running it than they did naming it. Sounds like they have gunfights every afternoon. That's better than bingo, I guess."

It occurred to him that it was probably not the best time to mention that the home would certainly have an activities director and a multitude of weekly events and trips that, if she were physically able, she would enjoy. There was for her in this moment, he knew, no comfort. Only loss.

"I want to know something, Pastor Martin."

"Pastor Martin? This sounds serious."

"Yep. Serious as a heart attack. Are you going to come see me?"

He thought of 250 miles between Kansas City and St. Louis on I-70, but answered immediately. "Of course I will, Annie. . . . Well, not every week. Maybe not every month."

She smiled. "Just once or twice. While I'm getting settled."

"You know I will."

"And will you bring that lovely wife of yours?"

"Mary-Martha? That lovely wife?"

She chuckled. "And your two daughters too."

"Well, coming and going that would be eight hours listening to Donna's pop music on the radio, Annie. So maybe I'll just bring Mary-Martha the first time."

"That would mean so much to me—"

The tinny, cellphone version of "A Mighty Fortress" rang in his pocket, interrupting them.

"I'm sorry, Annie." He held the face of the phone where he could glance at it, "A. Celeste" gleaming. "Can I tell them I'll call them back?"

"Of course."

He actuated the phone and pressed it to his ear. "Hi, can I call you back in ten minutes?"

"Can you come over in thirty?"

Larsen glanced at his watch. "Yeah, I think I can do that."

"Bye then." The phone went dead.

He dropped it back in his pocket. "Sorry about that, Annie. So impolite. Church business just finds you wherever you are."

An expression of great admiration spread across her face. "I don't know how you do it, Pastor. You keep up with all of us—all our aches and pains and bitching. And you never complain. At least I never hear you whining. And every Sunday morning you get up and lead us on toward heaven like we really were God's people instead of a bunch of snot-nosed crybabies."

He smiled, pushing aside the great feeling of irony her praise stoked in him. "Well St. Timothy's isn't all crybabies, Annie. And you're the farthest thing from a whiner."

97

She nodded. "Whining is exactly what I've been doing ever since you got here this afternoon, Pastor."

He set his cup down on the end table, the beginning of his ritual of departure. "We have talked about some problems you're having, Annie. But that's only because I asked about them. We just discussed your situation because I'm interested. Not because you're a crybaby. And I heard a lot of strength and triumph in what you said."

Annie stared at him. Was it an expression of joy or reflection she wore?

"I'm going to miss you, son."

Slowly he nodded. "I'm going to miss you too, Annie."

"Can we have a prayer before you go?"

This time the changes in the apartment could not be ignored. All furnishings, apart from the table and chairs that now seemed so insignificant, were gone from the living room and kitchen. With the blinds shut, the only light came from the ceiling fixture above the table.

Ange, wearing the little black dress she wore the first time he had come to her, watched him silently as he turned around, absorbing the dwindling presence of Joan Celeste and the growing implication that her daughter would be leaving soon as well.

"Can't say I like what you've done with the place."

"I'm returning it to its natural state: drab shadows."

He shook his head. "I always thought it was a bright, welcoming place."

"Yeah. Mom did that everywhere she lived."

". . . Not much left."

"Well. Out of consideration for you, I'm keeping the bed for last."

Larsen chuckled. "That is thoughtful."

"Something else I kept." She went to the refrigerator. "Seeing how I thought you might find this place a little depressing when you saw how empty it was."

She set vanilla ice cream, chocolate syrup and a jar of cherries on the table. A sweet, almost nostalgic feeling filled him. He pulled out a chair and sat down. Ange began to make their sundaes, licking her fingers, bending before him and tempting him to look at her untethered breasts.

"So what was it I called you away from while ago?"

"Umm . . . pastoral calling. I was visiting a sweet little old lady."

"You don't sound all that overjoyed about seeing her."

"Well . . . she's in a downward spiral right now. Annie's about to move across the state to a retirement home. In the process she's giving up her home of fifty years, her church, her friends . . . her car. And she has some physical problems that can't be fixed. She needs surgery to cure her degenerating spine, but she can't risk the operation."

Ange scooted a bowl in front of him. "I guess you deal with that kind of situation a lot."

"I do, actually."

She pulled out the chair across from him and sat down and started to eat her sundae with a girlish eagerness. "We have opposite problems, don't we?" She smacked her lips. "I mean, every day I try to get people to confront and change issues in their lives that are totally within their control, but they aren't willing to fix them. You on the other hand—" She licked the bottom of her spoon. "—try to comfort and empower people who struggle because they have creeping problems over which they ultimately have no control. Now that's why I could never be a minister."

". . . That's the best part, actually."

She straightened.

"No," he said. "I'm not saying it's any fun trying to lift up a person who is dealing with loss and decline they can never come back from. I'm saying that's the part of my job that makes you feel most like a minister and most useful. . . . When I was in college and seminary, I always imagined the part of being a pastor I would most enjoy would the preaching. I mean, I was good at it. People have always complimented me on my sermons. 'I don't know how you come up with a new message every Sunday, Pastor. And there's always something in the sermon I can take away home with me.'"

". . . All that praise got old for you?"

He chuckled. "What got to me was the realization that, even if people are listening, what you say in your sermon isn't going to make any real difference to them."

"Hmm." She grinned coyly and tilted her head. "Maybe your sermons aren't as good as you think."

"Yeah they are," he retorted. And when she glanced at him, he said, "Nobody gives sermon like me."

They laughed.

He sighed. "I think, after a while it becomes a bromide for the congregation. 'There's Pastor Martin in the pulpit again, so everything must be okay.' I've decided that, even if you preach something that's extremely prophetic—"

"What does that mean—prophetic?"

"Oh, like, if I preach that Christ is calling our nation to open its borders to immigration and calling our congregation to open its doors to minister to immigrants, that would be prophetic. Only if I preach a really prophetic sermon, most folks will come out and say, 'Your sermon was very stimulating today, Pastor.' 'You sure spoke from the heart today, Pastor.' Those are coded expressions that mean, 'Pastor, I appreciate your conviction and energy, but you should know that whatever you just said will not change my opinion, heart or behavior in any way.'"

He scooped the last of his ice cream onto his spoon and swallowed it. "True story and 'aha' moment. Back when I was in my first pastorate, we had the sweetest LOL you ever saw. She was just so sincere and gracious. She looked like Mrs. Claus, too—300 pounds and 5 foot tall. Pure silver hair. Every Sunday Mrs. Rawlings would come out of the sanctuary after church, shake my hand and say in the most sincere tone, 'Pastor, I so enjoyed your sermon today.'

"Well, her sister and brother-in-law started visiting the church and I made an evangelistic call on them. During the course of the conversation, Mrs. Rawling's little sister happened to mention that her big sister was stone deaf. She couldn't hear a word from more than ten feet away. 'Well does she read lips?' I asked. 'Lord no,' her sister says. The next Sunday after worship I'm standing at the back door and here comes Mr. and Mrs. Rawlings. She says, 'Pastor, I so enjoyed your sermon today.' I say, 'Why thank you, Mrs. Rawlings, seeing how both you and I know you didn't hear a word I said.' She breaks out laughing like a schoolgirl. Covers her face with her worship bulletin and scurries out." He sighed. "So much for preaching."

". . . Well. There's got to be something you like more than calling on the ailing sheep of the flock. What about weddings?"

"Oh, Christ! Weddings are the worst."

Startled, she giggled. "Oh. Glad I don't want you to do my wedding. What's so fucking wrong with them? Bridezillas?"

"More often it's mother-of-the-bride-zillas."

"They want to control everything, do they?"

"Well some do. Lots of MOBs forget—"

"An 'MOB' is . . . ?"

"'Mother of the bride.' Obviously."

"Obviously."

"Anyway, a big percentage of them forget it's not their wedding and they are not in charge. Ultimately if it's a church wedding, it's the pastor who is in charge."

"I can see how that would cause some friction."

He laughed. "Yeah. A friend of mine got really fed up with an MOB who kept trying to dictate everything. This went on for several months leading up to the ceremony. Finally, on the night of the rehearsal, the MOB decides to lay down the law about who's in charge. My friend gets real close to her and whispers, 'Mrs. So-In-So, if you don't back off, I'm going to ask you to leave the premises.' She says, 'You can't do that!' 'I certainly can,' he says, 'and I won't hesitate. You might look at it this way: if you aren't here tomorrow night, we'll have a beautiful, peaceful wedding ceremony; on the other hand, if I'm not here, all you have is drama in the parking lot.'"

She giggled. "That's too cool. You want some more ice cream?"

"No, thanks."

"That's good. I have something better."

"Anyway—" He watched her as she stood and put away ice cream and pulled two tumblers from the cabinet. "—another problem I have with MOBs is that they forget they're not supposed to be the center of attention. Like, when they try to personally cook a meal for the all the wedding guests or they try to be the wedding director. Your daughter's wedding is the worst time to be 'super mom.' It's also not the best time to wear a sexy dress and show your cleavage."

"I see." She took a bottle from a bare cabinet.

101

"What is that?"

"Sherry."

"Do tell."

"Yep." She began to wrestle with the cap. "I plan to get you liquored up and have my way with you."

". . . You don't have to liquor me up to have your way with me."

"Still. . . . It's fun."

". . . Well, like I was saying, I very seldom have much trouble with MOGs."

"Mother-of-the-groom?"

"Yeah." He leaned back in his chair. "Typically they don't create near as much havoc. Unless they're just out-and-out crazy. Or their ex-husband is there with a new 'arm piece' stepmother."

She poured the tumblers half full. "I can see that."

"Last year I had a wedding with a particularly immature MOB who kept calling attention to herself in inappropriate ways. She acted like a pouty sixteen-year-old. But despite how outrageous the mother of the bride behaved, the groom's mother stayed pleasant and quiet. So after the ceremony, as we were sitting through usually, interminably long picture session, I told the groom's mom how refreshing it was to work with her, especially in light of how much havoc the bride's mom had caused.

"She says, 'Well, the mother-of-the-bride has an awful lot to remember and deal with. The mother-of-the-groom only has to remember to wear beige and keep her mouth shut.'"

Ange laughed out loud. "So much for weddings. I guess funerals aren't that much fun either." She set the tumbler of sherry before him.

He shrugged. "If the circumstances are right, you can bring a lot of comfort to the family." He turned the liquor slowly in his hand, holding it up to the ceiling light to see the thick coating on the glass and took a first drink. "The bad thing about a lot of funerals is that you have to take care of the bereaved family, but you were close to the deceased yourself. You have to take care of everybody else without showing your own grief." He took a second sip of the sweet, tart liqueur. "And it gets worse the longer you're at a church, because you know people longer and better."

"That's really why I'm going back to Florida?"

102

"What?"

"Oh yeah. I live in fear that I'll get old and die and you'll get all upset my funeral. I can hear it now: 'Ange was not a religious person. She was cynical, smart-tongued and contentious. If she hadn't been so good in bed, I probably wouldn't have anything to do with her.'"

He laughed.

She smiled, topping her glass and then Larsen's. "I'm just trying to make it easy on you, Pastor."

"You're good that way."

"So do you bury a lot of your friends?"

"Well . . ." He took a long sip of the sherry, supremely sweet and hot. "I haven't had a lot of really close friends in the church. There have been a few. Like Barney Holder. You know, at every church I've served, there has always been one or two fellows who truly wanted to be good the pastor. I think it was a holdover from fifty or sixty years ago when ministers were—I guess the word is 'revered.' I've been lucky to have somebody in every church— well, everyone but this one—who went out of his way to be good to the pastor."

"Like how?"

"Oh. Like taking your family out to eat at a country club or a nice restaurant. Like going to the personnel committee at budget time and twisting people's arms to get the pastor a raise. Like taking you shopping for a new suit or getting you a brother-in-law deal when you need a new car."

She nodded. "And this Barney guy did this sort of thing?"

Larsen smiled. "Oh Barney Holder was the best. He was in my church in Dallas, the first one I pastored. Barney came around the first week I was there and took me to lunch and to an art exhibition. We were walking through the gallery. It had some magnificent pieces in it. And Barney says to me, 'Do you like this?' I say, 'Oh yeah, Mr. Holder. I think it's fantastic.' 'Yeah,' Barney says, 'I thought you'd like it. It's a little highbrow for me personally.'"

He laughed. "At that instant I knew we were going to be great friends. He taught Mary-Martha and me to sail on White Rock Lake. When Donna was born, he came around and told me to take two weeks off and asked if we had everything we needed for the

103

baby and for ourselves. . . . He loved baseball and, like me, he was an American League fan."

"American League?"

"Yeah. In Major League Baseball there are two leagues, National and American. Well the team in the Dallas area is the Rangers. And somehow along the way I got to be a fan of the Kansas City Royals, who are also in the American League. I swear, every time the Royals came to Arlington to play the Rangers, Barney got us tickets. And I mean just above the third base dugout."

"Is that good?"

"It's great. Real expensive seats. And he'd buy the concessions. The Rangers kind of sucked in those days, but the nachos they sold in the stadium were great. After half a serving of nachos with double jalapenos—about the time my belly began to feel like it was full of lava, Barney would flag down the beer man and buy me a tall, cold beer. 'You drink this, Pastor. I'm driving, so have all you want.'"

"Wow. He really was nice to you. So do you still keep in touch?" When Larsen's expression darkened, she said, "Oh, so he was one of those you buried. What happened to him?"

"Blastic myelogenous leukemia. . . . He just kept running out of energy. His skin got paper-thin. Couldn't catch his breath." He sighed. "Through this period of time, he refused to go to the doctor. His wife Marcy was on him the whole time, begging him to get checked out, but he wouldn't go." Larsen's chest rose and fell. "I think on some level he knew he was really sick and he decided to ignore it as long as he could. . . . Then one evening he developed a nosebleed that wouldn't stop bleeding. Marcy called an ambulance and then she called me. And I met them at Baylor." He nodded. "Took the doctors about an hour—maybe less—to diagnose him."

He tilted his head and stared at her. "That was a pretty damn awful moment, sitting there with Barney and Marcy. Neither one of them said a word. . . . So the doctor started talking again: 'We're going to do this test and that test and we're going to evaluate what treatment, blah, blah, blah. Barney cut him off. 'Doc, how much time have I got?'" Larsen's head dropped. "'Without treatment, three to four weeks.' 'And with treatment?'

'Two to four months depending on how you respond.'

"Barney just nodded, like somebody was telling him how much it was going to cost to repair his air conditioner or something. 'Can I go home now?' 'Oh, heavens, no,' the doctor says. 'You're going upstairs.' 'Yep,' Barney says, 'well I'm telling you now that chemo is out of the question. Why don't you just go make whatever arrangements you have to, Doc.' And the doctor left the room. . . . And matter of fact, Barney says to Marcy, 'Will you spend the night with me, hon?' And then he says, 'In the morning, I'm calling the kids all down here and tell 'em myself what's going to happen.'"

". . . He sounds like quite a guy."

"Yep. . . . He asked me to come back the next day after he'd had a chance to speak to his children. Marcy told me later on what he said to them. You'd have thought he was leaving on a cruise and was giving his kids instructions about what they were supposed to do while he was gone."

"Uh huh. How was it between the two of you after that?"

He stared past her into the darkened living room. He started to speak and stopped. Finally he said, "Marcy had gone out of the room for something. Maybe to make some calls. . . . I was sitting there alone with him, thinking to myself, 'You know, I'm trained for this. I know what I'm supposed to say, and I should say something. . . . But I—I just couldn't think of anything to say." He lowered his eyes toward the floor. "Then Barney starts telling me what he wants for his funeral. He clears his throat and says, 'Now let me tell you what kind of send-off I want, Pastor. Can you remember this or do you need to write it down.' I say, 'Barney, there is no chance of me forgetting any of this.' . . ."

Her voice seemed disembodied. He had no awareness of her posture or her appearance, only the gentle timber of her voice as she spoke. "How long did he live?"

"Eight days." He nodded. "Surprised everyone. I think . . . he willed himself to die. Barney always made up his mind and did what he wanted, what he thought was right. I sure wasn't ready for him to go, but apparently he decided he was ready. . . ."

"And you did his memorial like he wanted?"

"Exactly like he wanted. The scriptures he wanted. The hymns he wanted. 'I don't want A Mighty Fortress,' he said. 'We use that

105

way too much. Instead I want cheerful. Like "Joyful, Joyful We Adore Thee." And no 23rd Psalm. Every damn funeral you go to they read the 23rd Psalm. And I want you and you only doing my eulogy, Pastor.'"

Larsen found himself taking short, shallow breaths. It seemed there was heat behind his eyes and something on his cheek. He reached up and felt something wet.

"You really loved him, Pastor."

His head dropped forward and his breath became ragged. A low, deep moan he had never heard before rose from his chest through his lips. And Martin Larsen began to sob. His shoulders shook and he heard himself wail again. Then he felt her arms. They encircled him with a sweet, knowing firmness.

Eyes closed, he raised his face and wept. ". . . He was just so good. . . . He was just so good to me. And . . . I couldn't cry when I did his funeral. I couldn't cry . . ." He sobbed once more. ". . . for my friend."

He felt her breath on the side of his face as she spoke. Her voice was tender, consoling, accepting.

"It's okay, baby. It's okay."

Chapter Nine

"So from this text we glean, first, that the risen Christ did not withdraw from interacting with humanity following the resurrection. Second, we learn as well that there were those among his closest followers who struggled with their faith despite the magnitude of this miracle—or perhaps because of the incomprehensible grandeur of it; yet Christ accepted them even with their doubts.

"This brings us to a third lesson we may draw from this passage, one that's contained in one of the most famous verses in the Bible. Here the risen Lord imparts to his apostles what has come to be called 'the Great Commission': 'Go ye therefore and make disciples of all nations baptizing them in the name of the Father and the Son and the Holy Spirit.'

"It is fitting, I suspect that we are engaging this text today, the final Sunday of Eastertide with the celebration of Pentecost Sunday, the 'birthday of the church'—as it is so often called, the Sunday so closely associated with evangelistic growth—looming next week. Here we read the next-to-last verse from the Gospel of Matthew. Yes, here our Lord commands his closest followers to go forth throughout all the world and convert people from every land to our faith.

". . . Ironically, this verse is not only quite famous, but also extremely controversial, indeed in recent years this verse has been part of the polarization of the Christian faith. This Great Commission, you see, is often espoused as being the opposite extreme of another commandment from our Lord—also ironically found in Matthew—called the Great Commandment: 'Love God will all your heart, all your soul and all your mind—and love your neighbor as you love yourself.'

"On the surface there is no obvious contradiction between the Great Commission—to go and make disciples—and the Great Commandment—to love your neighbor as yourself. After all, if you recognize having Christ in your life as the most important truth of all, and you love your neighbor, then you want to share

107

your faith with your neighbor. Correct?

"Strangely enough, in the last seventy-five years or so, American Christians have refined and restricted our definitions of these two challenges from our Savior. The Great Commandment has come to be interpreted primarily as benevolent outreach; that is, Christ calls us to minister to those in need, those afflicted and hungry, those disadvantaged and displaced. Our denomination and those like ours—those called 'mainline'—have responded most positively to this commandment. Our theology proclaims that, every time we reach out to a refugee, every time we feed those who otherwise would go hungry, we are living out the Great Commandment.

"On the other end of the spectrum are more conservative Christians—denominational and non-denominational. Their great yearning is to proclaim the truth of the Gospel to all people, that every soul in every nation might know the name of the risen Lord and hear the story of salvation through Christ. These are the Great Commission people.

"Now, truth be told, we Great Commandment people don't have much use for the Great Commission. We tend to eschew evangelism. I do not misspeak, I fear, when I say that we look down our noses at folk who want to build mega churches and fill them with the previously unchurched. To us—and I think I do not overstate—that is an immature conception of our faith. And to be frank, we perceive that our evangelistic brothers and sisters, in bringing unbelievers into fundamentalist churches that hold mechanical views of salvation, are winning souls to religious beliefs that 'miss the mark,' beliefs that misinterpret just about all the essential tenets of our ancient faith.

". . . On the other hand, from the view of our Great Commission brethren, we are the ones who have missed the mark. They tend to believe that, in our refined, comfortable, well-educated theology, we have grown complacent about the one thing no Christian should ever take for granted—the soul of an unbeliever. To the evangelistic Christian, we have committed a great apostasy: we have ceased any significant effort to share our faith with those who have not heard the Gospel.

"And if I may be so foolishly bold as to be honest, each side is right about the other. Both Great Commandment and Great

108

Commission Christians—as my daughter Donna would say it— have committed an 'epic fail.' Today it's neither the commission or the commandment that is great—it is the division between us, the hypocrisy of our entrenched positions and our unwillingness to see ourselves as we truly are. . . . After all, here at St. Timothy and in all the churches of our synod and denomination, when we speak of evangelism we are primarily—well, solely—concerned with bringing in new members to our congregation so we don't have to worry about our church dying. And on the other side of the Great Division, the evangelistic Christians have equally missed the mark. As sacred as they may assume their duty to be, they are not about winning souls to a Gospel of freedom and empowerment, of grace and joy nearly so much as they are about creating religious clones in order to perpetuate the largess of their beliefs. Perversely, the unspoken goal of each group is the same—to attain assurance and comfort in the rightness of their beliefs. In reality, both sides of have failed to serve the risen Lord. . . . My friends, this absurdly clear.

"There is, however, a simple way to honor both positions; a way to be both a Great Commission and a Great Commandment servant of Christ. And that's what we're going to do here at St. Timothy's. We are about to become a mission church. . . . Yes. A mission church. We are about to start reaching out about us and serving others. No, we don't need to go Haiti to do this. We really don't even need to go to North Saint Louis. As I pointed out to the council when I brought to them the request that our congregation unite with a neighborhood development organization, there are a multitude of social needs we can meet right here in Manchester. There are schoolchildren right here in our city who go hungry every day. There are older adults living in dilapidated homes with no funds or physical ability to repair them. There are organizations striving to come into being that need an affordable, accepting place for regular meetings. Christ said to his disciples, 'I tell you, you will not go to every town before the coming of the Lord.' Accordingly I say, we will not meet every need that we can possibly address here in our little community before God's Spirit changes us all.

"And when we go forth in the Spirit, those whom we touch, we nudge, we brush with God's love will come here to bathe in it.

People will come to be with us in gratitude because they are astonished that we have discovered their needs and strived to meet their needs—on their terms—and asked nothing in return. People will come here in awe, to see what motivates this congregation to embody the compassion of our Maker. People will come here because they will want what we have. They will want to become servants as we have become servants.

". . . Now not everyone will be able to build porch ramps or to start food banks. So you'll be glad to know there are three ways to serve. First will be the workers: able-bodied, somewhat competent, at least willing souls who will go forth to embody Christ's love. I fall into that category, as does my very capable wife and my daughters—why are you looking at them? They knew what I was going to say. They're excited about this. They want to serve.

"There will be those who cannot physically do this work or who honestly do not have the time. That's okay. They can help pay for it. I'm going to ask the council to transform our evangelism fund into a mission fund. And I'm going to ask them to double that fund from our church reserves. That will be $2000 in seed money. Then I'm going to ask all those who are able to donate to this fund. So that once again it will be doubled. As we are deciding where to start our mission work, we will be building a fund of $4000 whose sole purpose is to enable St. Timothy's to reach out into our community.

"To be sure, there are those who cannot physically work on our mission team. Nor do they have funds to contribute to this work. Yet theirs is the most important contribution of all. They will be our prayer warriors. They will pray for the Spirit to guide us, to protect us, to bring fruit to our work as we go forth. . . ."

Larsen's hands had pretty much stopped trembling by the time he made it back to his study. His cheeks, he could tell, were still flushed.

What sort of response had he expected from his congregation, he asked himself as he unlocked the door to his office. The first ones out of the sanctuary had uniformly stared at him, or refused to make eye contact at all with him. He was, to these, a new person who had seized the body and pulpit of their pastor. They had no idea what to make of him.

Trailing behind the first group was a second throng who seemed totally unaware that this Sunday and this sermon had been different in any way.

"Enjoyed your sermon, Pastor," he heard again and again. "Dynamic preaching there, Pastor."

Then there was the third group, people who had waited intentionally to speak with him about his message. Perhaps two dozen all in all. Their enthusiasm had been electric. With them it was as if some long concealed, joyous yearning had been set free. As he shook hands and listened to the praise of some, others behind them in line began to argue about what mission projects they should undertake first. Larsen struggled to pay attention to those speaking to him while he could hear others who had already seized his ideas and begun to soar with them.

As he hung his cassock in the closet behind his desk, still reflecting on the potent comments of the third group, he had heard a firm triple tap on. Larry Looper stood just inside the door of his study, wearing a parental expression of disapproval. His jaw was set and his arms crossed.

"Pastor, I thought we had settled the whole issue of mission work at St. Timothy's. Is this your way of making an end run around the church council's authority?"

Before Larsen could respond, Looper was joined in the doorway by the diminutive form of Edith Kincaid. She was wearing a new outfit, trim and businesslike, well-suited to her short hair and the black-framed glasses on her nose. If she had heard Looper speak or had any indication that she were interrupting a conversation, she showed no awareness—or concern. Instead, with the slightest look of amusement, she immediately challenged Larsen.

"So, Pastor, this is quite a new initiative you're proposing. Actually, you know, you're not the first to propose new, 'earth-shaking' ministries—without consulting the leaders of the church or going through the committee process." She smiled cynically. "Actually in all my years here, I've seen it three or four times with three or four different, short-tenured pastors. Let's hope it works better for you in the long run than it did for them."

Larsen nodded. "Well, Edith, the truth is that the one actual leader of the church has been after me for some time to get off my

111

ass and inspire this little congregation to do anything that might be considered Christian ministry. In actuality, though, I'm really glad you stopped into my study. I've been meaning to tell you something with a witness present. And I think the Moderator of the Council is about the best possible witness."

"Witness?" A brief patronizing smile flashed again.

"Yes. Edith, you are hereby notified that you will never again go behind the back of the pastor to discuss with any other church member—or anyone in the synod, like maybe the bishop—anything that is said to you in the course of church business. For instance, if I tell you anything about my thinking or plans or intentions and you go to Bishop Johnson and tell him what I said or tell Mr. Looper anything we discuss in the office without my express permission, you will immediately be terminated."

Her position by the door and her posture scarcely shifted, but her countenance altered dramatically—from disbelief to awe to terror. In the few second he had spoken to her, she had gone from being the school principal to being the chastened child.

"Now I'm pretty sure I don't need to ask if you understood what I just said. Clearly you did. But to avoid any confusion going forward, I have already placed a letter to this effect in your personnel file and sent a confidential copy to all the members of the executive committee. I told them that they could come to me to ask for explanation if any was needed, but I don't expect anyone needs this explained to them. You have been throwing pastors under the bus for a long time. And somewhere down the road you may do it again. But if you try it with me again, you'll turn in your office keys immediately. . . . Do you have anything you'd like to say?"

She swallowed, but it was soundless. For half a minute she stared at him, too shocked to speak.

"That will be all then."

He turned to slip his suit jacket off the back of his chair and saw her hurry through the door and disappear. When he looked back up at Looper, the Moderator's face was pale but defiant.

"You can't fire the Moderator."

Larsen smiled. "You think you need to be fired, Larry? Concerning your snide little remark about making an end run around the mission work of the church, the council decided not to join a community betterment organization. What I was talking about in the sermon today had nothing to do with that."

"Still, you're trying to usurp the—"

"Back up, Larry." His voice was touched with a hint more anger than he intended. "Don't talk to me about being a usurper. You have torpedoed my ministry in more ways than one."

"How—"

"You came into my office not so many days ago and told me that people were complaining about my ministry. Remember that? You think it was difficult for me to figure out who you were talking to, to hunt them down and ask what their issues with my pastorate are? I had some really good discussions with Chuck Tarleton and Vernon Maxey. It was quite a learning experience listening to their take on your conversation with them about me as a pastor. They made it sound like you initiated the conversation— maybe even you were an instigator. . . . Regardless, Larry, even if it wasn't you stirring the pot, it's clear what you didn't do. You didn't say, 'You know, if we have problems with the way Pastor is leading us, we should go to him as Christian brothers and lay out our feelings.' You didn't say, 'We need to support our Pastor, and part of that is telling him when we think he's off base. We need to give him the opportunity to explain his intentions and goals to us. We need to be open-minded and honest in our dealings with him.'

"There is a saying about the pastorate, Larry, that in my experience is quite valid. I heard early on that in every parish where the pastor finds himself in hot water, the top lay leader in the congregation is weak. . . . St. Timothy's has good leaders to take care of worship, education, stewardship and even property. You have one job, Larry. And that is taking care of me. . . . You need to have my back.

"So here is how it's going to be. I have no intention of failing in this new mission imperative. St. Timothy's is going to go out into the little world of Manchester, Missouri, and witness Christ with its hands in a real way. And on down the road, church folks are either going to say, 'Wow, Larry Looper helped breathe life in the pastor's dreams.' Or they are going to say, 'Pastor Larsen succeeded despite the resistance of his moderator."

The men stared at one another. Then, as Edith had done before him, Larry turned and walked out the door silently.

Larsen leaned against his chair for a moment, wondering if he had just defeated his own goals with his plainspoken words. He pulled his keys from his pocket, stepped into the hallway and locked the office door. Mary-Martha and the girls had the engine of the minivan running as he walked across the parking lot. They stared at him as he opened the driver's door and got in.

"Was that Larry Looper?"

"Yes, dear, that was my moderator."

"Was he there to congratulate you on the most dynamic sermon you've preached since you've been at St. Timothy's?"

He turned to her as he buckled his seat belt. "Seriously? You think it was?"

"Everybody did, Dad." Daphne called from the pilot's seat behind him.

"You should have heard the grownups," Donna said.

"What were they saying? Was it good or bad?"

"It was amazement," Donna continued. "'What's got into the Pastor?' 'Would you do mission work?' 'I would do volunteer work in Manchester, maybe. I wouldn't go to the city.'"

"Ooo!" Daphne's voice was suddenly excited. "Can we do mission work in East St. Louis."

"Uh, no!" Mary-Martha responded.

"You're too young anyway," the older sister said. "You have to be in eighth or ninth grade to go on mission trips."

"No I don't. I don't, do I Dad?"

Larsen shrugged. "I expect it depends on what we're doing. If we're cleaning up neighborhoods and working at food banks, I don't think you're too young. Some organizations we might help, like Habitat, have age limits. You have to be like sixteen."

"That's stupid. I'm a lot better at manual dexterity things like sawing and hammering than Donna will ever be."

"Shut up. No you're not."

"It's not about ability. It's about insurance."

"Insurance?" Mary-Martha turned to him. "We have to have insurance?"

"We already have the insurance we need if we're doing a church project. But if we go on site for some other benevolent organization, like Habitat or a mission site organized by a denomination, we'll be covered by their insurance."

"That is so stupid." Exasperation radiated from Daphne's voice. "I'm a lot less likely to get hurt doing mission work than any of those hundred-year-old people in our church."

"That may be so, Daph, but those decisions aren't made by us church folks who are doing the mission work. They are made by insurance companies."

"Insurance companies?" Donna repeated. "Insurance companies tell you when you can do a church outreach project."

". . . Pretty much, sweetie. I remember when I was pastoring a little church in Dallas. It was about the time Daph was born. A church near us had a bunch of kids going on a choir tour—you know, where they spend a few weeks traveling around to different congregations singing. The day before they were going to leave, their old van broke down. So they called up and asked if they could borrow our church van. I said, 'Sure. Let me tell the property department you need it.' Well everybody in our church thought it was a great thing to do. Only, our insurance agent was a member of the church. He told us we couldn't lend out the van because it wasn't our church's choir that was going on tour. So we couldn't let them use our van."

". . . Did they have to rent another one?"

"No, Daph, they didn't have the money for that. The little church had raised all the money it could just to underwrite the trip. They didn't have anybody who could afford the four or five hundred dollars to pay for a van rental."

"So what did they do?"

"Nothing. They had to stay home."

"Stay home?" Donna was incredulous. "You mean they didn't get to go at all?""

"That's right. They didn't go at all."

"Because of stupid insurance?"

He laughed. "I think we don't realize it, but so much of the ministry that we do and can't do is dictated by insurance companies."

"That's like medical treatment," Mary-Martha said, gazing out the passenger window. "Ultimately it's lawyers and insurance companies making the rules about what doctors can do and not do for their patients."

"Oh, yes," Daphne echoed. "I see the unfairness of this. It's like parents making decisions about what videos and TV shows their daughters can watch."

"Or how long their daughters should be grounded," Mary-Martha said, her voice sly.

"Where are we going?" Larsen asked. "Are we lunching out today?"

"Pizza."

"You always want pizza, Daph. I want a burger and shake."

"Why don't you girls ever want to eat something healthy?" Mary-Martha spoke up.

"How about barbeque? We haven't had that in a while."

". . . I'm good with that, Dad."

He drove the van toward the interstate and St. Louis. A sweet, good silence descended upon them.

"I'd like to help old people fix their houses," Daph said at length.

"I want to buy clothes," Donna responded. When Larsen looked at her in the rear view mirror, she continued, "Not for myself. . . . We have these kids in school. They wear the same clothes every day. I mean, they have one or two changes of clothes. It's so sad."

"Well," Mary-Martha said, "they do have presentable clothes. Not everybody in the world does. But what about the families of those kids. If they only have a few clothes, what else are their families doing without."

"What am I supposed to do about that?"

"Well, you could get to know them well enough to visit in their homes and see for yourself."

"I don't think they'd go for that—a white bread girl like me, coming to inspect their personal lives."

"Well then your job is to figure out how to ask what they need. Without offending. Just maybe there are some small things you and the other kids in the youth group can do to make real changes in the lives of kids in your school who are going without."

"It has to be what they say they need, though," Larsen said. "You can't decide on your own how to help them."

Donna's eyes narrowed. "What do you mean?"

He drew a breath. "You know how wrong it seems that insurance companies can tell churches what ministries they can conduct and lawyers can tell doctors how they can treat their patients? Well, if you go into someone's house and discover that they don't have something that you do have and you think you couldn't live without, you will be tempted to make sure they get what you have. But maybe what you have is not what they want. Maybe there is something else they need a lot worse."

"Like you want to give them an iPod," Daphne said, "when what they really want is a microwave."

"Exactly," Larsen said.

Mary-Martha looked out the passenger window at west county skyline. "It's like my dad used to say. 'The church has never been very good at making people into Christians without making them into us.' It's not just that we expect people to take our faith, but also our culture. And our prejudices and our priorities."

"Well . . . I think if we do it right, we're as likely to be changed by our work as the people we're helping. . . . Maybe doing mission is supposed to be as much for us as it is for them."

Chapter Ten

She opened the door slowly, pulling it with her as she backed into the dark apartment. Larsen stood in the threshold, absorbing what he saw, the exquisite and the forlorn.

Ange leaned against the door, wearing the pure white, sleeveless nightgown he had seen before, briefly. It went almost to the floor, and beneath it she wore nothing. The rounds of her breasts were luminous in the dimness and the fabric embraced the curves of her hips and the slight protrusion of her vulva.

Behind her the room appeared to have been denuded of all furniture, all personal effects and all sources of light apart from the dull sepia that forced its way around the edges of the single, curtained window. As he followed her into the room, he saw on the floor beneath the window a palate of sheets and pillows on a thick bedspread.

Languorously, she closed the door behind him, turned the deadbolt and took his hand. They walked silently through the room to the bedroll. There, she pulled one shoulder toward her chest and slipped her arm out of the gown; then the second arm. The nighty shimmered as it slid to the floor and she stepped away from it and linked her arms around his neck.

Her lips and the heat of her breath had become familiar to Larsen. Even as he relished her taste and embrace, the realization this was the last time he would be with her—the feeling of emptiness—permeated the moment. He felt her fingers undoing his belt and the latch of his trousers and he began to unbutton his shirt. She moved back from him as he did and lowered herself gracefully to the sheets on her side, propping herself on one elbow. She watched as he took off his clothes and stood before her naked.

The corner of one lip arched in a half smile. "Well, Marty, are you just going to read the menu? Or do you want to eat?"

He laughed. As he knelt she turned onto her back and widened her legs, inviting his head to her lower lips. They were, he discovered with his tongue, already wet, and the passage behind them slick and deep. She arched her back, closing her eyes and rolling her head to the side. Within only a few, electric minutes, she sighed and began to rock her hips against the pressure of his face.

"Umm. Right there, Marty. . . . Right there. . . . Umm. . . . Umm. Oh, oh."

Ange pressed her legs against his shoulders and put a hand on the back of his head, forcing him hard against her pubis. Shivers ran through her for five, ten seconds, then she collapsed back onto the sheets, her arms and legs limp. Larsen sat beside her, marveling in the totality of her relaxation.

"So that's why you called me here today."

She laughed, her eyes still closed. "Oh, Marty. Fuck me now, baby." And she spread her limbs for him.

He knelt between her thighs and dragged his penis deliberately back and forth, dipping it within her labia and watching as his member grew thick. Unhurried, he entered her. She opened her eyes then, gazing into his, and wrapping her legs and arms around him, drawing him taut against her, holding him close so the only motion was the arching of his back and his regular thrusting within her. She moaned, her vagina tightening on him, and pulled his face to her, kissing him, forcing her tongue into his mouth. The stalks of her nipples rubbed maddeningly against his chest. Together—with the pressure of her feet on his buttocks—forcing him to push firmly against her, the sensation was irresistible, overwhelming.

"You're going to make me pop, if you're not careful."

"I want you to pop. . . . I want you to cum in me. . . . I want you to fill me."

"Oh . . . you shouldn't talk that way . . . because . . ."

He did not finish speaking, his words giving way to the explosive orgasm that drew him completely into her and, seconds later, sapped him of all energy. He lowered himself gently onto her, his penis throbbing within the engorged lips of her vagina.

They lay silently, his breath gradually subsiding, until at length he whispered to her. "Am I crushing you?"

"No, love. . . . I like the feeling of you on me. And in me."

Sooner than his body wanted to, however, Larsen rolled off of her and lay on his back staring up at the dull, featureless gray of the ceiling. He remembered that, after the first time he made love to Ange, the overwhelming feeling had been guilt, remorse. This day his feeling was grief, loss.

Again she propped up on an elbow, facing him. Her expression was casual. If she felt the sadness that gripped him, she did not display it.

"Be a good boy, Marty, and go see what's in the cabinet beside the refrigerator."

He did as she asked, ignoring—or maybe enjoying—the semen that slipped down his thigh as he walked across the room. The open cabinet door revealed only a bottle of the Nebbiolo he loved, a corkscrew and two wine glasses.

"You have class, Ange."

"Um hmm. Let's drink our sorrows away."

He turned toward her, the bottles and glasses in hand. "Are you sad, Ange?"

"Yeah. Aren't you?"

". . . Incredibly. It's just that . . . you don't seem to be hurting."

She sighed. "Well, in my experience, nothing dulls the pain of parting like a good fuck and a couple glasses of stout wine."

He chuckled and sat down beside her, his legs crossed. "I'll try to remember that. When I'm missing you like crazy."

Larsen turned the corkscrew and lifted and the bottle gave a liberated pop. He filled their glasses, pushed the cork part way into the neck of the bottle and set it in the window sill. Closing his eyes, he sniffed the wine and lifted it to his lips.

"What year is this? The wine, I mean."

"Beats me," she said. "Is something wrong with it?"

"Oh god no. It's wonderful. I love this Nebbiolo, but this is the best ever."

She drank a full swallow. "It is good. I never really drank this before, but I can see why you like it."

He stared at her. "What did you drink? Before you came here."

Coy light sparkled in her eyes. "Something stronger. Why?"

Smiling, he leaned forward and kissed her. "I know nothing about you, really. Yet somehow you seem to know everything about me. . . . Now you're about to walk out of my life and leave me without explaining yourself to me at all."

"Well what do you want to know?"

". . .Everything, Ange."

120

"Oh, no. We only have an hour or so, right? Then you have to go back to your nursing home people and your dysfunctional parishioners. How could I possibly tell you everything about me?" She studied his face, hers an expression of elegant, erotic wisdom. "And don't you know, if a girl gives it all up to her guy, he won't respect her in the morning. . . . I'm not talking about my cunt and my tits, Marty. I'm talking about my 'secret garden,' the place no one can go. . . . But on the other hand, I'm not a tease. So I'll answer—" She screwed her face to one side, as if in deep thought. "—three questions. Any three questions you have, I'll answer."

He considered his words carefully, then sighed. "Well then I'd better be damn careful what I ask, because you're going to be counting the question marks, aren't—" He laughed. "I almost screwed up."

She emptied her glass and poured it full again. "Ask away, pulpit boy."

". . . What made you decide to make love to me?"

Ange smiled. "Seduce you, you mean? Good question, because there is more than one answer. First of all, I had a feeling when I first met you that you were sexy as hell and inhibited as hell. You needed a really good lay, and I had a feeling I could help you out." She drank. "Second, I had the feeling that, if I did get into your undies, it would open you up to a whole new world of possibilities. I thought—hell—illicit sex just might empower you. And I was perfect for you in a way: no other attachments; only here temporarily; uninhibited." She held the neck of the wine bottle over his glass and filled it. "Second question?"

". . . Well, I don't think I got all the answers to question one, but I don't want to waste another asking for clarification. . . . So here goes. What is your opinion of me?"

"Ah! Another multiple answer question, damn you. What do I think of you? . . . I think you are sincere, a person of integrity—yes, despite your having an affair with me. I think you have a deeper spiritual life than 99% . . . make it 100% of the people you minister to. I think you are a bundle of power, confidence and ideals, just waiting to bust forth—like an orgasm—into action and achievement. I think you are open and inquisitive. A traveler and an explorer. I think you've chosen a career that disempowers you, but that you've reacted to that in ways that are brilliant—

sometimes anyway. I think . . . you deserve to have someone to watch over you and protect you."

An entirely strange, intoxicating feeling of awareness and luminosity washed over him. For an instant he thought of Paul on the road to Damascus, struck down by brilliant light. His head tilted to one side, he asked her an entirely different third question than he had intended.

"What do you know about God that you're not telling me?"

For the very first time in his knowing her, Ange's face showed dismay. The question truly surprised her. She considered her words now as cautiously as he had at first.

"Well. I did promise, didn't I?"

"Yes."

"Well. God is not a child. God does not hold against you the steamy romance we've shared in the last few weeks."

"That's good to know. But it's not much."

"I guess I can tell you that over the years, if you continue to seek it, the intimacy you have with the Holy One will deepen and the doors of communication will fall open. That doesn't mean the people around you will be open to what you have to teach them about God."

". . . And? How do you know this?"

"And that's question number four."

"Shit." He leaned back. "I'll make you cum for two more questions."

She giggled girlishly. "No. I'll make you cum and you won't have any more questions."

He shook his head, chuckling. "I'm afraid it's a little too late for that. For a few more minutes anyway."

"Oh, I don't know about that." Ange set her glass in the window sill. Unabashed, she leaned toward him and grasped his penis. "Drink up, Marty."

Her mouth descended upon his member with agonizing, magnificent slowness. It was like a kiss to him—familiar, hot, excruciatingly exciting. He was astonished that he grew erect almost instantly. As she felt it, she emitted a low, knowing moan. She leaned back from him and took the glass from his hand, setting it on the sill beside her. Then she pushed him backwards until he lay on his back, his head and shoulders off the pallet on the carpet and his tumescent dick flopping to one side. She straddled him, a silky leg on either side of his hips and reached behind her to guide the cock gently upward into her. As she sat motionless, looking down at him, her expression was mischievous, girlish. She tightened her inner lips, smiling at the jolt of surprise that wracked him.

Then she leaned forward, her hands beside his head and began to raise and lower herself onto him, her face shining with exhilaration. Desire. And some other emotions he did not recognize. Perhaps it was, he thought, her reaction to the bittersweet awareness that this fiery moment together was their last. And as if in response, she leaned forward onto him and kissed him, pressed her breasts against him and closed her eyes. They made love without speaking, as if each had decided to imprint the sensation of their coitus upon their everlasting memories.

She came. It was sudden and surprised him, arousing him irresistibly. Even though she slowed to allow the potency of the orgasm to subside, he could not. Grasping her hips, biting his lip, he forced himself upward into her. Then he came. After the thrilling burst, there was a moment—his eyes closed—when he felt completely disoriented. It was as if they were in motion, weightless, rolling together through alternating light and darkness. The sense of moving together passed in an instant, though he still felt displaced. He had to open his eyes to see if he were on top or still on the bottom.

She was looking at him, her face just above his. "You're a very good lover, Marty."

Ange didn't wait for him to respond. Instead she stood and reached down for his hand. He followed her to his feet and she led him into the unlit bathroom, leaving the door open behind them. She turned on the water in the walk in shower. This was something she had intended, he realized, looking at the two thick bath towels hanging on rack.

Larsen had used the bathroom several times since the beginning of their affair, but had never paid any attention to the shower. It was the barrier free sort with a seat and a shower head that detached. The splattering of the water was the only sound. In the half-light, he watched Ange leaning over the edge of the low wall, adjusting the temperature of the water. Her form, ungainly bent—like one of Dega's charcoals of bathing women—was nonetheless wonderful, symmetric, marvelously feminine.

She turned to him and smiled. "Don't worry, Marty." She took his hand. "I won't get your hair wet."

She guided him, childlike, into the shower. Detaching the shower head, she sprayed warm water over his chest and the front of his legs, then turned him and wetted his back and buttocks. She replaced the shower head and, his back still to her, poured a thick liquid on his shoulders. With a soft cloth she lathered his back, lifting his arms one at a time to wash his sides, kneeling to wash the backs and sides of his legs, reaching around in front to cleanse his still sensitive penis. She turned him toward her then. He watched her as she squeezed the soap onto his chest and began to wash him. They gazed silently into each other's eyes.

Larsen laughed and looked away, shaking his head.

"What's funny?"

"I was thinking, this is like being cleansed. Anointed. . . . In the gospel accounts, every time women anointed or cleaned the body of Jesus, either something really bad had happened, or was about to."

She pressed her wet, slick body against him, her nipples erect. "Well you're not Jesus, Marty. So don't go there." She took his hand and put the plastic soap bottle and washcloth in it. ". . . My turn." She turned her back to him.

He stood motionless for long seconds, then slowly encircled her with his arms, fondling her breasts, pressing his member against the curve of her buttock. And Ange leaned back against him, relaxing, her head against his chest.

He drew a breath. Holding the bottle above his palm, he squeezed soap into his hand and began to lather her chest, her neck and throat and slightly elevated arms, her stomach. When he felt the gentle half step as she spread her feet, he slid his fingers down to the protruding clitoris. She reached back and put her hand behind his head, moaning sweetly. He reached within her, his thumb pressed against her clitoris and a finger sliding within to the thick place part way up her passage. In response she bent slightly at the waist, her bottom pressed against him, her head drooping forward. She pressed her free hand on his, holding it in its tender embrace.

"Mmm. . . . Right there, Marty. . . . Touch me . . . right there."

Her thighs closed against his hand and, almost imperceptibly, she began to rock against his thumb and finger. Then came the quivering moment of climax, her limbs growing flacid. He put his arm around her belly to keep her from falling. For a full minute, she did not speak or move. At last she straightened and turned to him, hooking her arm around his neck and bringing his lips down to hers.

"Thank you, Marty." She kissed him again, a tender kiss of gratitude. "You're my love, Marty."

It dawned on him, as she reached for the shower head again, that they were both still lathered with soap. She rinsed him first, front and back, then rinsed herself and turned off the water. Silently she handed him the thick towel and stepped out of the stall.

"Let's go to another place, Marty," she said.

It took only a moment for her to dry herself and she left the bathroom while he was still wiping himself with the towel. By the time he came out of the bathroom, she was filling her glass with the remains of the Nebbiolo. She had pulled on the white nightgown.

"You have to drive," she said. "Not me."

"Okay. That's probably right. . . . What was that about going to another place?" Being naked when she was not somehow made him feel completely self-conscious. He began to dress.

She sighed. "You got to ask me three questions. It's my turn."

"Oh." It surprised him. "All right. Three questions."

"Nope. I only have one."

He pulled his britches over his underwear. ". . . Must be a doozy."

"Well, here it is." She finished the wine and set the glass on the sill by the empty bottle. "So, Martin Luther Larsen, there was this little war for your soul."

He stared at her, buttoning his shirt.

"On the one side was everything you had been totally invested in: a lifetime of moral behavior; faithfulness to your spouse; playing by the rules in church—even when the people who were busy dragging you down did not." She squinted. "Honing your ability to be the best pastor you could be within the increasingly

125

narrow confines of your ministry.

"On the other was me. Unselfconscious debauchery. Irreverent confrontation. Nothing taken at face value. Destroying those things you worshiped as precious. And making you feel guilty about what you had done, even though you couldn't resist coming to me. . . .

"So there was this battle for your soul. And I won. . . . And my question is, which side do I represent . . . hell or heaven?"

He stared at her. Momentarily he sat on the floor and put on his socks and shoes, then took a deep breath and looked up at her.

"I have no idea how to answer that question." He shook his head. "I really don't. . . . The longer we've been together, the less guilt I've felt. And I don't think it was because I got used to cheating. I think it's because I've begun to see things differently. . . . I always knew at the back of my mind that things weren't the way I built them up to be. You wouldn't let me lie to myself about that anymore." He shook his head. "I don't think this is a heaven or hell thing. . . . I think this is a 'wake up and be honest about what you know and what you believe' thing."

It seemed to him, despite the indistinctness of her features in the dim light, that his answer had some meaning to her. She held out her hand. He took it and got to his feet.

"When are you leaving, Ange?"

She nodded. "In the morning. I'm laundering the sheets and towels this evening. Then I'm giving them to Mrs. France, two doors down. She loved Mom's bedspread and I promised it to her if she'd take the sheets and towels too."

"That's good."

"And first thing in the morning, I turn in my rental car at the airport. My plane leaves a little after nine."

He studied her face. ". . . And if I need to get hold of you some day in the future?"

She smiled and shook her head slowly. "You won't."

"You don't think I'll want—"

"I don't think I'll answer if I see your name on my phone." Her expression was apologetic, but committed. "That was the deal from the beginning, Marty. You remember that. That's what made it work for both of us. I'm sorry to make you sad. It makes me sad too. Comes with the territory. I like to think our time together was worth it for you."

"Ha. Are you serious? It's been wonderful. Beautiful."

"That's good then." She smiled. "Mom would be happy."

"What? Your mother?"

"Yeah. Don't you remember? I told you after the funeral. Mom had some things she wanted to give the church. All those papers were for the congregation. . . . And I was for you."

"Ah. Seriously, I don't think your mom—"

Ange tilted back her head and laughed. "Don't underestimate my mother, Marty. You know how I conned you onto the chair to get those letters at the back of the closet."

"Conned?"

"Sure. I used a hangar to push them back beyond my reach so I could trick you into standing on the chair. Well guess what? Those were love letters. Between my mom and one of your parishioners. A married parishioner."

"What? . . . Who—"

"No, no, no, Pastor. You don't get to know that. It would surprise the hell out of you, though."

"Christ, Ange, she was in her seventies and eighties the whole time I knew her."

"The world is full of surprises, isn't it, Pastor Larsen?"

She stopped abruptly, her expression set. He realized suddenly it was time for him to go. His head drooped.

"Thanks," he said, "for everything."

"It was my pleasure."

She followed him to the door. They kissed before she opened it, just a gentle buss, a goodbye. Then she opened it quickly and light from the corridor flooded the apartment. Larsen pushed aside his desire to turn back to her and stepped into the hall.

"One more thing, Marty."

He stopped, gazing into her eyes.

"You always thought God was implying a judgment upon you—about the rat, I mean. You thought God was saying you were the rat in the church." She shook her head. "I don't think that was ever true. I never really thought the rat was all that bad. I mean, it turned the church folks upside down. And they probably needed that. I guess you could say the rat was more of a prophet than a menace. Even though, I think most real prophets are perceived as menacing." She pursed her lips. "I think it's more likely I was really the rat. . . . What do you think? . . . Love you, Marty. Goodbye."

She closed the door.

Larsen stood in the silence of the hallway for fifteen, thirty seconds. He sighed. She wasn't going to open the door again. And he wasn't going to be pathetic and knock.

The sunlight outside was brilliant. The friendly little Nissan was toasty inside and he drove away from Joan Celeste's apartment and quickly across the bridge into Missouri with the windows down, enjoying the freedom of the breeze.

Thoughts of Ange pressed upon him. He could not distract himself from the image of her standing in the dim apartment, the gown floating to the floor, revealing her marvelous naked form. It was her exquisite nakedness he was thinking of when his cellphone rang and he held it to his ear.

"Hello."

"Dad?"

"Yeah, Daph."

"Mom wants to know if you still have calls to make or you have to go back to the church."

"No, actually." He glanced at his watch. "I guess time got away from me. I'm coming home now. It'll take me twenty minutes."

"I'll tell her. . . . We're having spaghetti."

"Meatballs or meat sauce?"

"Meat sauce. Mom says you don't share when she makes meatballs."

"She just need to quit being so stingy with the meatballs. Salad?"

"Yeah. And garlic bread."

"Works for me. See you in a few."

"Bye."

Larsen smiled and slipped the phone back into his pocket. And once again he thought of Ange and their goodbye. Just as he pulled onto westbound I-270, it dawned on him that he had never told Ange there was a rat in the church.

Chapter Eleven

This time the heavy footsteps stopped outside his study, followed instantly by a firm knock.

"Come in."

The custodian opened the door. "Okay if I come in, Pastor?"

"Yes, Horace. Please do. How are you?"

"Fine thanks. Okay if I sit down?"

"Sure."

He scurried, almost childlike, to a seat facing Larsen's desk. "Well, Pastor, I come to make an announcement."

"You came to tell me you caught the rat?"

"No." Horace shook his head slowing, his eyes down. "Just the opposite, Pastor. That's what I have to tell you. The rat is long gone."

". . . Seriously? You don't think it just went to Florida for spring break?"

Horace smiled. "No. Don't know where it went, but no one has seen hide-nor-hair-nor-flea of it for a week now. All those traps I set out—not a one disturbed. The creature is just gone, Pastor."

"Well I would say that's good news, Horace, except you seem so downcast."

"Yeah. Yeah," he said slowly. "Not sure why I could never catch him, Pastor. He was a smart one for sure."

"Maybe so, but if you ask me the smartest thing it did was get out of St. Timothy's. Eventually its brazen misbehavior was going to catch up to it."

"I'll be ready if it shows back up. That's for sure." He looked up. "There's something else I wanted to talk to you about, Pastor."

"Yes?"

"You know those mission projects you was talking about in the sermon Sunday."

"I do, yes."

"Well, any idea where those will be? Out of town?"

"Uh, no actually, Horace. I'm friends with some other pastors

129

and churches and community organizers who do this kind of work right here in Manchester all the time. They're getting together a list of projects we can work on."

"What sort of work then?" He rubbed his chin.

"Well we can choose. There are lots of household construction projects—"

"Like fixing kitchens and bathrooms and building ramps and such?"

"Yes." Larsen nodded. "Painting projects. Drywall work. Putting in new floors. Tearing out landscaping that's run wild. General clean up. Adding barrier free rooms. Porches. You name it."

The custodian pursed his lips. "Well, me and the missus talked it over. We'd like to be part of that."

A strange warmth came to his face, intense behind his eyes. Larsen gritted his teeth, surprised and elated and trying not to weep.

"I think that's wonderful, Horace. You would be a great addition to our mission team. Didn't you used to do that kind of thing for a living?"

"Yeah. Was foreman of a general contracting crew. Know how to do just about any kind of work like that."

He nodded. "And you think you can show other people how to do it?"

Horace shrugged. "Nothing to it."

". . . That's so serendipitous. So great. We need someone who can show us how to do things the right way." He smiled. "That will be strange. You'll be the boss of me. And Mary-Martha and the girls."

The custodian considered him closely. "Don't have to pray or anything, do I?"

"Oh no. Not at all. That's one thing I'm actually pretty good at. I can pray with the best of 'em."

Horace nodded. "Think we should now?"

"Dad. You got to let me on your computer now."

Larsen looked over his shoulder at the matter-of-fact expression of his older child, who stood behind him, pressing a thick notebook against his back.

130

"Something wrong with your iPad?"

"It's not hooked up to the printer. And I can't type on it."

"Oh—" He rose in mock haste. "Well let me get off my site and out of your way. Just what is it you have to write and print?"

"This is my French One term project. I have to do a report."

She settled into the chair before the computer and immediately opened a page to an on-line music service. High pitched pop began to play. Larsen leaned down, put his hand over hers on the mouse and lowered the volume.

"In French, sweetie? You have to write it in French?"

"No. The report can be in English."

"That's nice."

"It's about a French artist from the Romantic period."

"I see."

"The Romantic artists shared the same epoch the Neo-Classical French artists, the late 18th and early 19th centuries. These two schools of art theory, however, are not to be confused."

"Perish the thought."

"The Neo-Classical artists—you know, like Jacques-Louis David—were throwbacks to the realism of the ancient classical artists."

"Oh, of course."

"Don't tease me, Dad. The Romantic artists, the most famous of whom was Delacroix, were more focused on the power of nature and natural forces, the point of which was to find ways to portray emotion and the human condition." She gazed up at him. "You going to stand there?"

". . . No. So who are you going to write about? Renoir."

"Oh, god, Dad. He was an Impressionist. You are impossible. You knew that, right?"

"That I'm impossible? Or that Renoir was an Expressionist?"

"Impressionist! I've chosen to write about Rene Marie Collette."

"Seriously? . . . I would guess women artists were pretty rare back then, even in France."

Donna turned to him again, her mouth open in agitation and disbelief. "Are you still putting me on, Dad. He was a man. With a beard and everything."

"Collette Rene—"

"Rene Marie Collette."

"Donna, he had three girl names."

"He was a guy, Dad." Her voice was indignant. "Now go away."

Larsen moved away from her and slid onto the couch. He took the remote and turned on the television.

"Don't turn that up loud. . . . I'm trying to concentrate and it interferes with my music."

"Music? Is that what you call that?"

He muted the volume and scrolled through the sports channels, looking for an American league baseball game. When he could not find one, he began to flip through the news stations. He had not realized before that he could follow the reports with the sound off.

"Want to see him?" Donna called.

He glanced at the monitor. "Sure."

"This is a portrait of Collette when he was, I guess, about thirty-eight or nine. Isn't that how old you are?"

He craned to look at the screen. "Yep."

"He looks older than you."

"Beard makes you look older, I guess. How long did he live?"

She studied the information on the website. "Real old. Seventy-four."

"Um hmm," he said. "That ain't real old." He began to surf the cable channels again.

"And here is an essay about his most famous painting," Donna continued. "*Ange Descendant.*"

He started. "What?"

"'Descending Angel.'"

He straightened and look at his daughter. "What is it in French?"

"*Ange Descendant.* Descending Angel."

". . . Ange? Descending Angel?"

She nodded. "It's real neat. Want to see?"

An odd fullness swelled within him, lifting him from the sofa. He stepped behind his child and looked over her shoulder at the image on monitor.

The painting was a large landscape, swirling with amber, red and light blue. The earth, the lower three quarters of the canvas was dark, troubled, windswept. The male figure at the bottom, slightly to the right of center, was obviously in distress. Even with his face turned away from the artist, the peril and angst he felt were palpable. His arm and hand, reaching skyward, were bare and pale. And descending from the left of the painting, reaching down for him, borne on gilded, magnificent, luminous wings, was the angel, her shimmering robes flowing behind her to reveal her bosom and lithe form. Her descent—or perhaps the great wind that troubled everything else in the painting or perhaps the air current created by her wings—forced back her long, black tresses, revealing an oval face with perfect features.

". . . Have you seen her before, Dad?"

He steadied himself. ". . . Yes. Yes, I have."